Whiskey with Wolves

MASCOT BOOKS
an imprint of Amplify Publishing Group

www.mascotbooks.com

Whiskey with Wolves

For more information, please contact:
Mascot Books, an imprint of Amplify Publishing Group
620 Herndon Parkway, Suite 220
Herndon, VA 20170
info@mascotbooks.com

Library of Congress Control Number: 2023921925

CPSIA Code: PRV0124A
ISBN-13: 978-1-63755-836-2

Printed in the United States

To my husband, Shane, who loved me
back to life.

And

to Maw-maw, my Wonder Woman,
who made me as smart as I am strong.

With a special thanks to Jeff for helping
me see my potential as a writer.

Whiskey with Wolves

A Novel

ERICA SPRAY

MASCOT BOOKS
an imprint of Amplify Publishing Group

Prologue

"Are you ready, Sadie?" Andy asked.

That was a loaded question. "Am I ready to testify against the man who helped build my career? I don't even know how I got here."

"How you got here is a miracle." Andy's eyes were serious, but his tone was loaded with compassion. "Most people don't walk away from this amount and level of abuse."

"I didn't walk; I crawled."

"The most important thing is that you made it out," he said. "Your testimony alone could lock up your abuser for a long time."

Forever wouldn't be enough for him.

"Collect your thoughts, Sadie. Find a starting point you're comfortable with and go from there. Your story is important. The whole world should know."

When I heard the word *abuse,* I had to think about it. Abuse was so definite. Was it abuse I suffered? Was it torture? Was there a difference? There is no scale for abuse that says what one person endures is greater or less than what another may have experienced. Abuse is immeasurable.

Even though I knew what I went through was wrong on every level imaginable, I still sat on the fence on whether I somehow deserved everything that happened to me. Did the last seven years of gaslighting rob me of my sanity and desensitize me from my trauma? Had the years of isolation, manipulation, and lies caused me to believe my life had been normal up to this point?

These questions spun inside my head as I prepared to make a statement to my attorney. I was about to explain in great detail several years of mental, emotional, and financial abuse given to me by someone who promised to always keep me safe. I had to decide if I should participate with his ongoing investigation or take the money and run.

My thirtieth birthday was just behind me, and I had nothing to show for the last ten years of my life. With him, he took my youth, my spirit, my confidence, my self-worth, and what little faith I had to begin with. My bones were holding up the shell of a woman where a young, bright, vibrant woman once stood. I refused to make excuses for him anymore. And I was done trying to save him. The FBI was now involved with the case. Beauregard Franks was going down with or without my help. One thing I learned over the last few terrifying years: keep your friends quiet and all your enemies clueless.

"I'm ready to tell the truth," I said, more confidently than before. And when the anxiety wrapped around me like a straitjacket, I whispered to myself, "I can do this. I have to do this."

CHAPTER ONE

Stranger from Home

"I'll have a Red Wolf, and he'll have the same," he said as I pulled my strands of auburn hair out of the beer cooler.

You need to rotate the soon-to-expire beer to the top of the well while tending bars in no-name little towns. You have to do everything yourself. But I was used to that.

His voice was attractively deep and full of cockiness. I noted his all-too-familiar southern accent was Texan. But when I looked up, his accent was the last thing on my mind. His beautiful and mysterious eyes nearly made me drop the glass I was holding. But I could tell there was a lot more lurking behind the sparkle in his deep blues. I thought I recognized old pain.

I certainly didn't mind his debonair and rugged looks. He was tall and semi-well-dressed, almost like he had money but didn't know how to spend it. His outdated gold jewelry looked like something my Sicilian grandfather would have worn. But the chiseled jawline beneath his burly beard belonged to him.

"Hello? Can you hear me?" his friend said while answering his phone. "Dammit! There's no reception in this Podunk shithole!" He stormed back out.

"Here's your beer," I said, trying not to sound interested in any way. "Would you like to start a tab for you and your friend?"

"Naw, I got cash," he said with a smug look.

There was the accent again. I remember thinking he had to be on a vacation of some kind because he ordered a fruity red lager, and the sun had not been kind to his skin. A bottle of Red Wolf is like a Corona. If you aren't sitting on a beach, it sticks out when you order it.

"What part of the South are you from?" I asked while counting back his change. When I started out, it was hard for me at first to hold a conversation and count money. But when you're on your own, and your job is your life, you learn to do both well.

"What makes you think I'm from the South?" he asked, pretending I was wrong.

"Your cowboy boots, for one. And that unmistakable accent, for two."

"I'm from Tyler, Texas," he said with elongated vowels. "You know where that is?"

Ironically, Tyler was roughly an hour and a half away from my hometown in Shreveport, Louisiana. How was that even possible this far north? I guessed right then and there it had to be fate. "I do. You're a long way from home. I guess you're on vacation?"

He took a swig of his beer. "Naw, just here on business. Do you always greet your guests like this? Or am I special?"

I snickered, wondering what kind of business Red Wolf was into the way he was dressed and drinking on a Tuesday afternoon. "I'm from Shreveport. Your voice reminded me of home a bit."

"Well, young lady, you sure are a long way from home too." He took another swig, until the bottle was empty. "But I don't hear your accent at all."

"I spent a lot of years getting rid of the twang in my voice. I'll thank my speech therapist for you." I walked to the other end of the bar and started cleaning the glasses I had cleaned thirty minutes prior. "Here in Oklahoma, they'll make you read the menu just to hear your accent."

I wanted to know more about him, without coming across like I was interested. And I had a cocky attitude at that point in my life. I knew some of the men feared me. I liked that. And they all wanted me. I liked that even more. And a female bartender can't take shit from anyone, unless you want each night to be a living hell. If you don't lay down the rules from the start, the drunks get bolder, and your butt gets slapped harder.

So I told it like it was to whoever was buying. Most men liked it. They flirted with cheap pickup lines, and I would shut them down. I was harsh just to make my point, but funny enough to make their friends laugh and keep them coming back for more. I got famous in the little city of Thackerville for my one-liners. It wasn't long before I got regulars, and quite a few came just to see me.

"Thackerville isn't exactly a hotbed of big money," I said while reaching for a dry towel. "It's just a lot of trees and a big casino."

"It's what's underneath that matters," he said in a *I could care less what you think* tone.

When you work a bar long enough, you learn how to read people. The drunker they get, the easier it is. Except for this guy. Red Wolf, my nickname for him, was a mystery. Every time I said something to get more out of him, he didn't bite.

As I turned around to ask if he wanted another beer, he was heading for the exit with his friend's beer in his hand. I was surprised, to say the least. I'd gotten used to being hit on by every hard leg that walked through the door. Red Wolf was different right from the start, more so than anyone I'd ever met.

He had me second-guessing myself the moment he didn't hit on me. I wondered if I'd lost my charm. I went to bed that night wondering why a mysterious cowboy from Tyler, Texas, was in Thackerville, and why he didn't even ask me my name.

I was twenty-two years old.
I was craving adventure.
I was desperate for a life that I couldn't remember.
I met you that day, and you sold me a life.
You sold me a way out, oh, and I paid the price.

CHAPTER TWO
Young Sadie Crowe

I WOKE UP ON ONE OF MY DAYS OFF with the sunlight right in my eyes. And whether I liked it or not, Red Wolf was first in my thoughts. Like the sun, it was pleasant and annoying at the same time. I couldn't shake him out of my brain. I laid there with lazy thoughts, wondering about my past.

I never thought of myself as a runaway. It was more like I always felt abandoned, forced to make decisions on my own. I left home when I was seventeen. I wasn't running from anyone or anything, and there was no intended destination. And there are certainly many children in this world with worse families and backgrounds than mine. But constantly being left alone at a young age creates what I call *forced courage.* My heart knew there was a better place for me out there, far away from Louisiana.

Abandonment can take on many forms. I never knew my father or his side of the family. And my mom was always in and out of my life, so I spent many days and nights with my aunts or my grandparents. Like everyone, I yearned for attention and love.

When people say they don't need those things, they've likely just hardened their souls after being denied and hurt too many times. Don't get me wrong—my family loved me, just not in the way I needed. They refused or didn't know how to show affection. To this day, I can't recall a single time my grandfather told me he loved me. He didn't need to. It was unspoken but shown through his consistency. We didn't hug or discuss feelings and emotions. When my feminine emotions came alive, I had no idea how to cope with them.

My grandmother's nickname was Maw-maw. She was always tough on me yet instructive in her own way. She brought some Cajun flair to Shreveport, although it was on the northside of Interstate 10. Maw-maw might not have been the nurturing type, but she taught me I could be a pretty girl and street-smart at the same time. Her lessons help me even to this day. I wish I'd paid closer attention when I was a teenager.

Yet I was always alone and dealing with hurt feelings. That's when the shadow of alcohol crept up on me. I was a willing victim because I just wanted to feel numb. I couldn't fix what was broken, and I couldn't fill in what was missing.

As a family of non-Christians, we didn't pray before meals. We didn't hug or hold hands. We kept to ourselves and never asked for help. I had a couple of friends who lived near the river, and their families didn't have a lot of money either. And my friends and I didn't own fancy video games or even a computer. I didn't really understand the concept of college until I was in middle school and overheard my best friend, Renee, talking about it.

We played outside unsupervised until the streetlights came on. But we had better stay out of trouble in the meantime. And if we drank from the garden hose, we needed to turn it off tight when we were done, or we'd endure my grandmother's wrath. There was no running in and out of the house either. An air-conditioned home was a luxury. I can still hear her say, "Better not let out the bought air!"

I was in high school before I realized I had grown up in a shady section of town. It might have been the main reason—there were probably more—I never had sleepovers. My friends lived in nicer areas, and their parents would never let them spend a single night at my house.

High school was always a battleground to me and still is. It resembles *Lord of the Flies* increasingly with each generation. I was already at a deficit with a mostly missing mother and a father unknown. I never felt good enough, smart enough, or pretty enough to my peers. So that meant popularity was damn near impossible.

I was pretty, but not like some of my debutante classmates. My figure was mature for my age. And I might have received more attention with a better wardrobe. Stylish clothes were not in the family budget, and I had to wait until I could afford to buy them on my own. Even my shoes were ratty old hand-me-downs from the older boys in my family. Being rough around the edges led to me being a target for bullies. I was never going to be perceived as the typically sweet and innocent little girl that society expected me to be. All I wanted to do was fit in somewhere so no one could know my weaknesses and insecurities.

I had experience in something other kids didn't. Alcohol was new and daring to most of my classmates, but not to me. That made me a bit cool when they found out. All parents let their kids take a sip from their drinks, but I got to experiment far more because I was alone almost all the time. Our house was always fully stocked with beer and bourbon. We may not have had money for new shoes, but we always had money for whiskey.

In Shreveport, tourists only see the casinos and riverfront restaurants. There's a ton of fun things to do around the casinos and lots of great greasy food. When I was little, with no money to spend, I used to watch the boats drift by, wishing I could hang my feet over the water. There was fun to be had if you had money. But tourists never saw the ugly underbelly, where hard men, like my grandfather, worked the docks. If it weren't for them, most of Louisiana would starve. It was a dangerous job; therefore it paid more than most for those without a college degree.

One of my earliest memories of alcohol was when I turned seven. My grandfather and his work buddies had finished unloading a big shipment and were having one of their monthly union meetings at our house. They would all come over to drink heavily and discuss politics while they listened to rowdy country music.

My grandfather was a dedicated worker yet also a poster child for functional alcoholics. He worked all day and drank all night. He drank all morning on the days he was off. In my head, I can still hear him saying, "You can't drink all day if you don't start first thing in the morning."

My grandfather never let his alcohol get in the way of work and vice versa. He used most of his extra income buying beer and refilling the keg he had outside. To this day, I think Grandpa was prouder of the kegerator than he ever was of me. Most Americans have never seen or heard of a kegerator. He took an old fridge and converted it into a beer tap. Then he placed the keg in the fridge to keep it cold. The last touch was drilling a hole for the spout on the outside. I'm quite sure the kegerator was the main reason our house was chosen for the crucial union "meetings." Without their dirty work gloves, they had beer or liquor in their callused hands at all times.

Their wives would come too. They'd be in the kitchen smoking cigarettes and preparing snacks for the men. All of them wore long polka-dot dresses and made certain their big hair had been pulled up in what everyone called a beehive. The men stuck to beer or scotch, but the wives drank vodka or flavored rum mixed with fresh fruit juice from Maw-maw's garden.

"Who wants another salty dog?"

Every time I heard Maw-maw shout that out, I ran around in circles, looking for an actual puppy dog. At seven, I was smart enough to catch on. I asked my grandmother for a sip. And that particular time she was drinking coconut rum mixed with pineapple juice. As soon as the rum hit my lips, I felt the burning, sweet sensation. It was one of the most delicious things I had tasted to that point. No wonder they always sat around and drank. From then on, I wanted to be like them, look like them, and drink like them.

I was thirteen years old.
I was lost and afraid.
I sipped on the idea of running away.
I sipped on a little more than the wine.
I sipped on a life I was desperate to find.

CHAPTER THREE

Running Nowhere Is Still Somewhere

ALMOST SEVENTEEN AND DRINKING with my friends under the bridge near the river was a big moment in my early life. We had ducked out of school for the hundredth time, which always seemed like a good thing to me. I'll never forget the water that afternoon. The brown waves were angry and let the rocks on the ledges know it. When I think back, it was a warning sign about the direction my life was going. But I was too lost to see it. I wasn't interested in anything other than getting out of that town.

A few of the older and cooler girls were plotting a hasty departure from Shreveport. They were working out the details of packing up and leaving in the middle of the night sometime after graduation. When they let out they were heading to the West Coast, they saw my face light up. They were seniors, but I was only a sophomore. When they invited me to go with them, it was a no-brainer.

I left a note for Maw-maw, but I didn't tell my other friends about it. I thought it was cool how we were all leaving without a trace. We drove away at midnight on a random Sunday night. I sat in the back seat drinking my fifth beer, knowing I would never go back to high school. And I didn't care. People usually say that when they mean the opposite. Not me. Not then. I just wanted to see what else the world had to offer besides the rough and hollow life I was living.

It took us three days to get to the Pacific Ocean. When we got there, I was stunned by the beauty of the blue water. I figured every ocean was like the Gulf of Mexico. Please don't get me wrong—the Gulf has its own nostalgic beauty, but nothing compared to me standing on the West Coast sand with my toes submerged in the cold water of the Pacific. I cried. It was like standing in water from a movie. I didn't know it was possible to feel that way about a place, and I doubted I would ever leave.

Two of the girls and I lived out of the car for the next six months. That may sound like a depressing situation. But I felt like I was the richest person alive. I was free, with no one to tell me what to do. I could go where I wanted, when I wanted, and drink while doing both.

I smiled every time I walked on the Hollywood Walk of Fame, and I visited the Chinese Theatre all the time. It may sound crazy, but even though we slept in a car on the edge of a park outside Los Angeles, I felt safer there than I ever did in the house I grew up in.

I remember having panic attacks while sleeping at home. The older I got, the heavier the weight pressed on my chest when I slept in my childhood bedroom. It was an unfriendly shadow lingering in the room whenever I woke up in the middle of the night. I never knew what caused the panic attacks, but the pressure on my chest went away when I left Shreveport. And I've never returned to sleep in my childhood home.

The freedom I experienced was new and wonderful. We made just enough money while working at a movie theater. We always took the late shifts and holidays that no one else wanted. We partied when we got out and slept as late as we wanted.

Just past our seventh month, Catherine, my closest friend in the group, announced to us she was leaving. And I was devastated. I didn't want the perfect world to end. Then she invited me to go with her. Her older cousin in Oklahoma could get us both fake IDs and could teach us to bartend. Most importantly, she wanted me to be her roommate. When you grow up without the compassion and attention of a healthy family, your heart feels like it's starving. And when you let alcohol shield you from the specter of abandonment, you'll reach out to anything or anyone who gives you an ounce of affection.

A few days later, we said our goodbyes to our other friends, who had crazy aspirations of making it big in Hollywood. All of us were young and free, and no one could tell us how foolish and dangerous our choices were at the time.

We headed to Thackerville, a small town in Oklahoma just north of the Texas state line. That's where her cousin worked. He was dorky and not very cordial, but he was business-smart and owned his own bar. He needed our help because the Sturgis bikers were coming through in a few weeks on their way to South Dakota. And they always stopped at his place because the beer was colder and cheaper than it was at the Winstar Casino. When he told us we might earn more than $7,000 during the days they would come through, my mouth hung open for several minutes. That much money, at that point in my life, was like finding buried treasure.

Catherine and I learned all we could about bartending and helped out with whatever her cousin needed. And I found serenity within the wilds of Oklahoma when I went for walks. It was everything the beach wasn't, but in a good way. I wanted to connect with nature, as it was my new higher power. Endless farms and fish-filled streams, with crisp, clean air, distracted me from the fragmented bustle of the modern world.

One strange thing I discovered about myself while bartending was that I drank much less while working, even though I was always surrounded by alcohol and drunks. Catherine and I had many happy memories, feeling free and strong. I started becoming a better version of myself in Oklahoma. I was surrounded by a group of peers who wanted to live healthily. I don't mean they just chose to eat healthy foods. They were also spiritually and emotionally healthy. I found it refreshing to be accepted for all that I was without being judged for all that I wasn't. I had been raised in an uglier environment, where people made racial slurs on their twelfth beer by noon on a Friday. Leaving my home and life by the river was the best decision I made. And I decided I was never going back to that small, ignorant place.

A few of my new friends were attending college in Oklahoma City and seemed like they were really going somewhere in life. They were goal-oriented and career focused, yet they never made me feel inferior. In fact, they were a bit jealous because I was making good money for my age, and bartending was a job you could take anywhere.

Catherine taught me how to drive—a debt I could never repay. When I turned twenty-one, I got my driver's license, so now I had a legit ID and could drive where I wanted without being afraid of getting pulled over. I was inspired to get my GED, but I couldn't work up the nerve to ever take it. I knew a college education would help me achieve my goals, so I promised myself to start socking away tips and drinking less for the next year. I set a goal to save enough cash to pay for my first semester at the community college in Oklahoma City.

In the meantime, I could put off taking the GED until I was serious about taking the next step. The cost of living was low in Thackerville, and I was back in touch with nature. Life really seemed to be giving me a break. Somehow I'd wound up in a simple, happy life, content within my thoughts and emotions. I could finally see the rays of sunlight piercing the gloomy clouds of my upbringing. That's when Beau Franks walked through the doors and wrecked my perfect world.

The sky is the limit on passions unknown.
But encouragement dies on the other end of the phone.
You couldn't see me living in a faraway land,
with my dreams and future spontaneously unplanned.
I don't mind wandering free.
I'm careless at heart.
I have nothing to finish if I never start.

CHAPTER FOUR

Beau

I've always had a sense of exploration in my blood. I often wondered if I inherited this trait from my biological father. I never knew him. I suppose that's why I continue to believe the happy lie he shared a positive quality with me. None of my other family members had the wandering itch or even left the area for business reasons. The gravity of your hometown is strong. It takes a dose of wanderlust or a certain set of circumstances to leave for good.

It was kinder and less painful on my childhood heart to be convinced my father's absence was due to his own wanderlust. Facing the harsh truth he bailed because he didn't want me was too difficult to manage at such a young age. Children who experience such a brutal start, orphans especially, often bury the ugly truth to survive emotionally. I'll always have a soft spot for people who never had parents. It can be devastating to any child's psyche, to have their hearts broken early on. It can be a difficult wound to heal. Even today I feel strange admitting the first man who broke my heart was someone I never met.

There was no denying I loved wandering around the country, collecting friendships and experiences I could use for my poetry. Nothing was more relaxing after a long day's end than a glass of Johnnie Walker, a bath, and writing poetry. I believed the words flowed from my heart and soul when I was drinking. I liked to picture myself as a female Hemingway, producing my best work as a belligerent drunk. Maw-maw adored the singer Glen Campbell and claimed she loved his voice and music before his songs became popular.

"He was drunk at every concert," Maw-maw said. "And it never hurt his music one bit."

Conversations like that can sneak inside a child's brain like a hungry fox lurking around a henhouse at night. At the time I couldn't comprehend why she felt the need to justify a person's alcoholism to me at such an early age. Yet there I was, ten years later, justifying my own harmful drinking behavior. Rationalizing that whiskey helped me write poetry allowed my conscience to avoid the reality I was becoming an alcoholic, if I wasn't one already.

I needed to drink to keep myself calm when I was left alone with my thoughts. Alone in your own head is the scariest place on earth, in my opinion. So that night I did what I do best: I slipped into something comfortable, I poured myself a large glass of scotch, and I wrote.

I still have the diary, if you can call it that. Every once in a while I go back to it and read one particular entry I wrote about God's purpose for me. I didn't even know God at the time, and what I wrote was far from his purpose for me. It wasn't until I was on my knees, praying for my life, that I found God. It was there, at the edge of my world, he showed me all that I had gone through was the path I chose. And the most important part of everyone's path is that you wind up in the right place.

The path of drinking at an early age happens all over the world. But no other state knows alcohol quite like Louisiana. It's not a cliché. It's a mentality you learn as a child. Maybe that is why I was bold and rash enough to leave home as a teenager. There's something different about Louisiana that makes alcohol look fun and glamorous. My grandfather's union meetings taught me all the wrong things. You better hold your liquor in the South, or you'll get ridiculed into tiny little pieces. I think I had a love for scotch because of my maternal grandfather. But the truth is, I just loved the attention I got from men when I ordered it. "Now that's a woman who can drink," they would say loud enough for me to hear.

Now that I'm older and far away from Shreveport, I realize my relationship with alcohol was never normal. My surroundings had a way of normalizing the behavior. Some of my earliest memories are from attending baby showers with hunch punch. At every young child's birthday party, the adults drank heavily, played horseshoes, and had more fun than the kids. And there's nowhere else you travel to that holds a weeklong celebration in which people drink heavily all day, then drive around town throwing beads and candy at strangers.

It's one of the traps about alcohol. I'm not condemning or judging anyone who drinks. I just believe things would turn out better if the whole story were told when kids are old enough to understand. The fun side of drinking is easy to spot. But no one tells a young girl that half of the homeless population in big cities is a result of "too much fun." No one shows you the households destroyed or the affairs that lead to divorce or violence.

No one ever explained to me the bad side of heavy drinking. It was as common as tying your shoes. I didn't comprehend as a kid that alcoholism not only existed but thrived throughout my family. And the worst part of the unhealthy environment I grew up in was that no one led me to believe I could become anything more than a smart-ass bartender.

Beau changed all that. That was Red Wolf's real name.

"Sadie, unlock the doors," the cook said as he headed into the kitchen.

Every morning at 11:00 a.m. I turned the latch, wondering if Beau was going to show up at my bar that day. Throughout a two-week period, the drinking cowboy had popped in a few times. He always claimed he came to see me. I fought hard not to let on I was flattered.

Beau Franks was the type of guy who was told too many times as a young boy how attractive he was. It usually spoils men. They believe it and use it to their advantage for the rest of their lives. Most young women handle the adulation differently than men. No matter how sincere or true the compliments are, women have a way of allowing insecurities to erode their own confidence. Then they hand out false compliments of their own, and around it goes.

Maybe it was simply the South's good-ole-boy's system that's pervasive there to this day. Although southern women yearn for compliments at an early age, they're taught their place in a man's world. Maybe it's everywhere—maybe since the beginning of history. Most women blush when they receive the compliments they long for. But when they're alone with their thoughts, they'll dismiss them as people just being nice. I learned the hard way that confidence, or the lack thereof, can have a big impact when two people meet.

I could tell from day one Beau was accustomed to getting the attention he wanted from the women he spoke to, wherever he went. I refused to give him the satisfaction, which made him try harder. And that excited me.

He acted shocked and insulted when I didn't eat up his every word. It might have seemed like the sassy bartender had the upper hand, but I still couldn't read him. I could never be certain if he was telling me the truth about anything at any time. He would go on with bravado about all his adventures, traveling the country as the head honcho for a real estate development company. He mentioned money a lot and never missed an opportunity to toss in how much of it he made.

In my experience, people with money never let on they have money. But I didn't say that out loud. His name was Beauregard Franks. "Everyone calls me *Beau*," he said. He proceeded to tell me he was in Oklahoma overseeing a multibillion-dollar construction project and had a large crew doing all the work for him.

One afternoon he mentioned he was looking to hire someone sharp to assist him with his day-to-day tasks. Beau wanted a personal assistant the entire field personnel could utilize. For a split second, I considered myself for the job. But I quickly dismissed that idea after I glanced at my *GED for Dummies* book on the floor under the bar. The hair stood straight up on the back of my neck. Another divine sign I missed.

I didn't think much of the comments after that. Until then, I'd never met anyone who had an assistant. I even suggested a few people I knew who may have qualifications. It never dawned on me that I was capable of being an assistant or that someone like Beau would even consider me as a candidate for such a venture when I didn't even have a high school diploma.

The next time he was in the bar, he asked me why I was in Oklahoma. I explained to him I was the lone-wolf type, a nomad of sorts. I learned not to long ago that lone wolves in the wild eventually cross into another pack's territory. Then they have to deal with the pack leader. If the lone wolf is accepted, it joins the pack. If not, it is chased off or killed.

"I've never belonged to anyone or any place," I said, passing him another beer.

Beau was surprised by my comment. He assumed I had chased some boy halfway across the States, and then he dumped me. He was surprised to learn I'd been brave enough to leave home, all on my own, and start a new life for myself at such a young age.

I was twenty-one and somehow convinced myself I was both mature and streetwise. But now I know I was just a vulnerable kid with a lack of purpose. Like many before me, I was lost, not even knowing what I was searching for in the first place. I found missing pieces of myself in the strangers at the bar. Longing to be loved and feel whole made me an easy target.

I'm convinced Beau could tell right off how broken I was but wanted me to believe he thought I wasn't. I was too lost and full of myself to see he was crafty and sinister. He never missed a chance to carry on about how much he loved my banter, or how witty and smart I was for a girl my age. Beau handed out enough compliments in one day to overinflate my ego for two months, tricking me into believing I was better and further along than my peers. Worse, I fell for one of the oldest lines in the book: *You're different from all the other women I've ever met.*

I loved hearing how mature I was from older men. It was human nature for someone like me in that position. But I was clueless as to how immature I actually was, ignorant of the manipulation tactics men like Beau used on unsuspecting and naive women.

Beau had a sly way of flattering me. He didn't fill my head with the typical compliments. He would comment on my attitude with gusto. *She's a firecracker! I need a wise girl like you out in the field to put those hands in their place.*

I loved feeling like I was in control and that I could manage such a task. The possibilities started to percolate.

I'm acting out of character
from what I've often done.
But I'm feeling more mature this time.
I'm not leaving just to run.
It's getting colder, and I'm lonely.
But what should I have to fear?
I'm changing as a person
with the changing of the year.

CHAPTER FIVE
The Starving Soul

It was a fateful Friday afternoon when Beau walked in with a couple of his work buddies, and he was holding some papers.

"Red Wolf?" I yelled out to him.

"You know me so well," he replied with a crooked smile.

The crew went to a table, as it was dinnertime. The Friday-night waitress would have her hands full with them, but she would be tipped well. Beau didn't sit with them. Instead, he walked straight to me.

When you are romanticizing someone early on, you don't see the hungry teeth within the smile. You only look at the surface and dream.

"Ya studyin' for a test?" I asked while pointing at his papers. That was the first time in a long time my Louisiana accent slipped out.

"Not quite," Beau said. "But I'm glad you brought that up. Today is the last day for us on this project. But we have another project kicking off in thirteen days."

Another omen I ignored.

"Where are you headed?" I said, hiding my anxiousness. A new project meant I might not see my Red Wolf ever again.

"The next one will be near my old stomping grounds around Caddo Lake in Louisiana."

"I thought you were from Tyler, Texas?"

"Well, my shit of a dad moved us when I was a kid. We were ninety minutes from Texas Stadium, where the Cowboys played. Anyway, enough about all that. I came to see you because I think you should come work for me."

"Work for you?" I was puzzled and flattered.

"Yeah, come work for me. Be my assistant. I could use someone sharp and confident like you. And from what I can tell, you are educated plenty enough. Do you know Microsoft Office?"

"Who doesn't?" I said with a bit of sass. "My generation grew up with computers."

"Me, for one. I don't know computers. See, that's why I need you."

"But I already have a job." I looked around the small-town bar in Thackerville, Oklahoma, trying to convince myself this place was where I was supposed to be.

"Come on, Sadie. No offense, but this place is a dump. A bright girl like yourself can do a hell of a lot better than this." His tone was stern this time. He slid the papers across the bar to me.

"What's this?"

"Salaries," he said with that same grin. He ran his finger down the list of names with all the wages next to them. He rested his finger on the position I assumed was his.

Project manager, $250,000! That's what I yelled in my head while acting coy.

"And this one would be your job and salary." Beau pointed to the position labeled "Asset Administrator," with the corresponding salary.

"One hundred thousand dollars!" That one I yelled out loud. I was shocked to the bottom of my shoes. I never dreamed anyone in my family could make that kind of money in one year, especially me. "Let me get this straight: You want me to quit my bartending job so you can hire me as your assistant? With a company I know nothing about? And you're going to pay that much money? And there aren't any strings attached? That all seems too good to be true. And why me?"

He'd finished his Red Wolf already and was about to leave. I knew all his mannerisms by that point. "I've got a good feeling about you, kid."

When he called me *kid*, I got goose bumps because I felt like anything but a kid. Ilsa Lund from *Casablanca* played out in my head, with Beau saying, "Here's lookin' at you, kid."

"Let me think about it," I said, trying to give my spinning thoughts a chance to take it all in. "I'll need to do some research."

"On me or the company?" Beau looked a bit hurt or vulnerable.

I couldn't tell if he was being shy or faking it. "Both," I said with a smirk.

That night I called Abby. She was my first best friend. She sort of helped me grow up in a way because she was a little older than me and kept me under her wing. She loved me unconditionally, and it showed. She was my person, my coconspirator, confidant, and the only one I trusted to be totally honest with me no matter the topic.

"There's never a bad time for a job offer making six figures," she said.

I couldn't argue with that, especially for someone like me, who'd never been exceptional at anything until bartending came along. My sassy persona engendered a reputation of a girl with confidence, someone put together. But it hid the reality that I was incredibly insecure and afraid of failure.

It's hard to tell when the fear of failure began. After I dropped out of high school in tenth grade, I was too afraid to take the GED. I was smart enough to pass it. I don't know why I never took the test then. At the time I didn't need anything or anyone to keep score on whether I was worthy of success or not. If I ever planned to pass it, college was the obvious next step, and that seemed farther away than the moon. But I wouldn't need a college degree with the job he was offering.

"Do you trust him?" Abby asked.

"I don't even know the guy." That was partially true. It stuck in my craw that I knew a lot about him and not a damn thing at the same time.

Abby sighed. "Okay, do you sense he's a good person based on what you do know?"

"I don't suspect him to be a horrible person. I just can't figure him out. On one hand, he seems like a professional, put-together, genuine guy."

"And on the other hand?" she interrupted

I shook my head, though we were on the phone. "On the other hand, he strikes me as the type of guy that if you spent one wild weekend with him, he would wreck your life forever."

"Okay, so don't spend any wild weekends with him," Abby replied.

Abby's response was far more logical than my mother's. Her

initial response was filled with the drama of a Lifetime movie. She seemed overprotective, which I found ironic, considering she didn't raise me. But I still valued her opinion even though she always assumed the worst.

"He just wants to use you, Sadie. No successful, honest man pulls a young girl from a bar and offers that kind of money without wanting something in return."

And she would know. I'm pretty sure the reason my grandparents raised me was because she ran off with some magician she met in a bar. Oh, how history repeats itself. Minus the creepy magician part.

Maybe she is right, I thought. Why would anyone want to hire me? I didn't feel special. And I certainly didn't believe I warranted a business proposition like that. I wasn't qualified and had no education.

Right then and there was my biggest mistake. My soul knew the truth. Hells bells, even my mother knew it. I could smell something fishy. But I ignored it. And it would cost me more than I could've ever imagined.

When I didn't hear from Beau that weekend, my insecurities went into overdrive. It was ludicrous to think he was serious about offering me a job like that. *He had obviously changed his mind,* I kept telling myself.

By the time Monday rolled around, I had accepted and rejected the job offer at least fifty times in my head. My heart raced when I saw Beau walk through the door of the little dive bar I called home.

"Good afternoon, young lady," he said with *the* grin.

Maybe it was an inner defense mechanism that made me blurt out why I shouldn't accept the job offer. "My mother doesn't think your intentions are pure."

He shrugged. But not in a casual way. It was a shrug that conveyed he didn't give a crap about my mother's opinion and wouldn't stop until he got what he wanted. "That makes sense. I can understand why any mom would feel that way. I have children of my own, you know?"

I didn't know that. He always asked about me, and I rarely asked about him.

"You're a dad?" I asked.

"Yes indeed. I've got two girls and a boy." That unassuming smile slipped across his handsome face.

"My mother also thinks you only want to sleep with me." This I said with more swagger. It was more akin to my barroom banter.

"No offense to your mother, but I've slept with many women." His eyes gleamed when he drew out the word *many*. "And you can tell her I have never offered any of them a job making *at least* a hundred grand."

"At least?" I asked.

"There's often perks when a job goes well. If the land is ripe and my crew does the job neat and tight, we get more money. All of us."

"So why me?" I wanted the real reason for his invitation—what he saw in me.

"Like I said, I just have a good feeling about you. I trust my instincts. The boys say I've got a good nose for these types of things. This is simple. I need to hire someone. And I think you are as good as anyone I've come across in a long time."

"Okay," I said with caution while inside I swooned.

"Okay, what?" There was that tone again. It wasn't a growl, but it was close.

I forced a smile. "Okay, I'll come work for you. I'll be your assistant." I didn't know I'd just started building the avalanche that would eventually bury me. I hedged the decision, thinking I hadn't signed anything. I could back out if I changed my mind. I would bartend and be content.

Beau didn't hide how pleased he was with my acceptance of the offer. "That's great! I'll have Reese get in touch with you. She's the lady in the office who will help you fill out all your hiring paperwork and go over the juicy details. I've gotta get goin' now, but we'll talk soon. And I'll bring over your company phone, computer, and business cards because that's what you'll be using from now on. Oh, and Sadie, you won't regret this." Beau winked at me for the first time as he walked out the door.

I downed a shot of whiskey before the door clicked shut.

Cloud nine had blurred my judgment. A company phone? Business cards! It took only a moment to go from rotating beer in a cooler to having office supplies sent to my apartment. Who would I give them to? Would people be calling me for things?

For the first time in my life, I felt like I had a chance for something bigger. This could be my way out of the uncertainty of being a young girl from the South whose only two options were to build a mediocre career without a college education or stay home raising babies. Neither of those appealed to my wandering spirit and a soul starving for recognition. Beau believed in me. He saw the potential hidden underneath the background I'd kept hidden from the whole world. It was my time to shine.

The reason I'm miserable
lies deep within my heart.

I don't want to explore those emotions.
So I don't know where to start.
Yet I'm running from my demons,
wherever they may be.
But now there are demons in Louisiana,
because the demon lives in me.

CHAPTER SIX
The Lure of Real Money

"WHAT AM I DOING HERE?" I asked my apartment full of unpacked boxes.

I was back in my home state, a few hours' drive from Shreveport. During my years away, I had kept in touch with my mom and Maw-maw enough to let them know I was safe and alive. I knew I had burned some bridges because of the way I left home, but I repaired what I could.

Accepting the job with Beau had me on edge. My emotions were tangled in knots, mainly because I had no idea what I was doing. With the added expectations of a real job that paid real money, I needed a few glasses of cheap scotch to calm me down. I drank to my heart's content while I made the new apartment habitable.

The commute from my apartment to the jobsite in Caddo Lake was under thirty minutes. I was able to pocket a good portion of the up-front paid-travel money given by the company every month. I learned so much in the first week of my new job. I felt professional, powerful. And for the first time in my entire life, I felt accomplished.

My office was inside a portable building in the middle of a jobsite. It certainly wasn't the glamorous setting I had anticipated. But that made me feel more at ease when I got there. I didn't have to wear typical business attire either. They let me wear nice jeans, an oxford-style button-up with the company logo on the left pocket, and steel-toe boots. I even put on a hard hat when I left the office.

This was quite far from the corporate picture Beau had painted. Yet it was a relief for me. I worried through several bottles of liquor the first weekend because I knew I wouldn't fit in with educated ladies in a fancy office. That's not who I was. But I settled into my new duties without a single problem.

Throughout each day, the men from the jobsite would find their way to my office to ask questions about their paychecks. They claimed their reason for seeing me was to make sure I had been clocking their overtime hours accurately. One of the nicer ladies in the office, closer to my age, teased me because they wanted to check out the new pretty girl. I didn't mind the attention.

Some of the guys on the Lake Caddo site were young, fresh-faced boys. And others were older men with weathered skin from working so many years in the sunlight. I couldn't figure out why anyone would willingly work in the terrible heat day in and day out. Then I saw the size of their checks, and it all made sense. Where else could a boy fresh out of high school bring home six figures?

The company rewarded the older men who couldn't read or write just as generously. And there were plenty of them wherever we went. The older men had been trained as teenagers to fix and work on bulldozers and excavators with their fathers rather than going to school. Most were illiterate but were experts at maneuvering heavy equipment, a valuable skill in the industry I was now a part of.

I tried to learn as much as I could as fast as I could. Every site I went to during my days with the company were simple landscaping jobs for the contractor, many times from Japan or China. They were buying up property in the United States and outbid everyone most of the time. There were many times we stayed on the sites to uncover what was under the ground for the contractor. If there was oil, natural gas, or a place good for fracking, there was extra money for us.

We used sensory equipment, and if we found a hot spot, we did the digging. Any person capable of digging inches from an underground utility or loaded gas line without striking it was highly sought after in this field. It wasn't something you could learn in college or trade school.

Other than hard labor and experience, being lucky enough to know someone who would teach you the ropes was the only way into the field. Being an equipment operator was as good as gold. The kids and grandkids of the older men were the next generation of construction workers. They would often end up in management positions by working summers with their fathers. In a few years, the younger men would wind up with both education and experience. They'd become top project managers and estimators. Like almost all industries, it really mattered who you knew. But my company even more so—it was exclusive.

The last group on the jobsites were the silver-spoon boys who hadn't had to work a hard day their entire lives. Their fathers either owned the company or owed a favor to someone who wanted their son to get his foot in the door of an oil company. Oftentimes these young men had a college education from a prestigious university, majoring in business or finance management. I had a rough background, but I wasn't bitter toward others. I always thought, *Good for them.* But the regulars on the site loved it when those types came out to the field. They heckled or belittled the silver-spoon boys for going to college rather than straight to work. The crew would call them all kinds of names as if they were not real men, because they didn't have tough skin and calloused hands.

Spencer was considered a silver-spoon type. He was Beau's boss and never knew a thing about construction until the owners hired him after an internship. Although he received a costly education, he wasn't afraid to get his hands dirty when necessary. Beau respected him because of that. He was eager to learn, and rightfully so. If Spencer played his cards right, he could end up in the vice president's seat one day.

Like anywhere else, politics played a major role in the industry I had joined. Construction and real estate were scrutinized by a lot of people and regulators over who was purchasing and the motive behind it. And maybe that was the reason everyone in our company seemed to be related or connected. The company was like an elite club you had to be invited to join. Throughout my years with the company, I never knew anyone who had applied to work there. Everyone had been invited by someone, like I was.

There were a lot of peculiar things I noticed early on. Some were obvious. It didn't take a genius to notice all the men in the field had one thing in common: they were all white men. And the women in the office, also all white, were not as respected by the men. We were females, and we lived in the shadows of a real man's workplace. What separated me from the rest of the ladies was that I understood the day-to-day field operations, and the other women didn't. It also helped my standing that the men in the field respected me.

I was the only person who brought the office to the field and vice versa. So it didn't take long for all the guys to feel at ease with me, knowing I could help them read and fill out forms. I was smack in the middle of the chaos of digs and land surveillance while making sure everyone sent in the required documents. Daily footage reports had to be sent to upper management. And without someone like me out in the field, none of that would get turned in. The workers weren't lazy; they just weren't educated and didn't know how to get the tedious part of the job done. So that's where I created a niche for myself and became invaluable to the whole operation.

The paperwork I handled allowed the office to track all the costs, production, and losses. I considered myself lucky. I was more valuable for having both field and office knowledge; this explained why I got paid a generous wage.

Working with Beau was great when I started. He was funny and charming. He picked me up every morning and let me ride with him to and from work to save on gas. At the time, I drove an old Ford Bronco with worn-out mud tires on it. It was the first vehicle I ever owned. Just after my second year in Thackerville, I'd saved enough tips from bartending to buy my first car. I was proud of my baby Bronco, but the gas mileage was terrible.

Beau shared stories with me on our way to work. He was hyperfocused in the morning, fueled solely by caffeine and the pills he took for weight loss. And I say solely because I rarely saw him eat. He was the first man I ever met who was concerned with his weight. He always talked about how jacked his arms "used to be" and how dieting would get him back into shape. I thought it was odd behavior for a man who carried himself with such confidence. Yet I had the luxury of a twenty-one-year-old metabolism, which I later found out doesn't last forever. But his vanity made no sense to me.

The drives home were my fondest memories getting to know Beau. As soon as we pulled away from the jobsite, he'd pull over so we could get into his cooler full of beer and down-home punch. We'd drink the entire way home, belting out country music at the top of our lungs. Sadly, for my ears, he sang as if he had an incredible country music voice. He would sing Randy Travis songs, convinced he sounded as good if not better. I never had the heart to tell him otherwise.

My boss and I driving home drunk in a company vehicle should have been another giant red flag, but I was having fun, so I let that one go. And that's a slippery slope. My cautionary advice to the younger generation is that the bottom of that slippery slope isn't fun at all and not for the fainthearted. If only I could go back and warn the sassy, naive bartender from the river.

Somehow our twenty-minute drive from the jobsite lasted almost an hour. I was usually half drunk while he turned down wrong roads because he was more drunk than I was, or it was on purpose. Sometimes we detoured to the casinos in Shreveport, where we would take in a few more drinks. We both enjoyed gambling. For some reason, Beau loved slot machines.

Then I taught him how to play stud. It surprised him how I kept track of the hands. And I wasn't a card counter by any means. I watched with horror one night when a guy was taken to the alley, never to be seen again. His third offense was unfortunately his last.

On the evenings we stopped at the casino, we would play for hours. Sometimes we talked about our love lives, the ones who hurt us, and the ones who got away. The alcohol made us more open. I had just ended a six-month on-and-off relationship with a guy ten years my senior who'd acted more like a bratty child than a man. When I found out he had cheated on me, we were done. It was months before I found out Beau was married. I was shocked when one of the guys from the crew let it slip out at lunch one day. Beau gave him the evilest look for saying it. What alarmed me was Beau had him fired the next day for being late. Another danger sign I ignored.

"You're married?" I said when we took a break from the card table and got a bit of food.

"I'm separated, Sadie . . . it's complicated." Beau refused to look me in the eye.

Another enormous red flag waved in my face. It was one right after another. Most people don't stay together anymore. And I had no reason to believe he wasn't separated. At that point in time, he hadn't lied to me about anything else, so I let that one go too.

"After all the stories I have told you, I can't believe you never told me you are married."

That's when I saw his feral look for the first time.

I was quick to amend my comment. "Separated. You still should've told me."

"I didn't think it mattered," Beau said.

"Tell me everything!" I acted like a ditzy schoolgirl demanding some juicy gossip.

"There's not much to tell, really. I met her in high school. I wanted to leave her then, but I got her pregnant. And the rest is history."

"Why are you separated now?" I asked, feeling a bit sorry for him. I was grateful he was showing his vulnerable side.

"The kids are almost grown, and we agreed when they were a certain age we would go our separate ways."

"Wow, she seems so cool and understanding. You're lucky. Most married couples hate each other through the divorce process."

"I wouldn't go that far. I'm far from lucky, considering what I've been through with her. She is jealous and crazy. She's just a dumb bitch, to be honest. I can't wait till we're divorced."

I absolutely despise it when a man calls a woman crazy. The good-ole-boy system created this uneven misconception. It's a comment that raises their status to judge and jury, as if there are no crazy men out there. And there are more than enough bad actors on both sides who do horrible damage to families. But somehow it's always the women who are labeled *crazy*, while the men are just *boys being boys*.

He slandered women in general, and he never saw the looks I'd give, or he did but chose to ignore them. Another red flag I ran past. I wasn't a Taurus, but my spirit animal must've been a bull because I don't think anyone has charged into that many red flags without stopping once.

"Sorry, I just get emotional when I talk about the situation. She trapped me, and now she spends all my money. That's why it's a sore subject. So let's talk about something else."

"Stud!" I yelled. The conversation made me feel vulnerable, and I was an avoid confrontation kind of girl. I'd just won a big hand with double-downed kings and queens, and the house busted just at the right time. We didn't talk much about his wife after that.

I may be back in Louisiana, but I made it just in time.
This time of year is my state's time to shine.
Festival season is only a few days away.
And when the cat isn't home, the mice will all play.
The music, the food, the weather, the lights.
The only thing I missed in this city were nights like tonight.

CHAPTER SEVEN
Dancing with a Ghost

My life had changed for the better in so many ways, but I still felt like the odd ball out. Deep in the shadows of my inner fears, I was waiting for the hammer of bad luck to fall. Every day Beau dropped me off at the office trailer I breathed a sigh of relief it hadn't turned into a big corporate building. The less sophisticated the work environment, the more comfortable I felt.

Most of the ladies were nice to me, but they were educated, polished, and ever politically correct. They called me the "fly on the wall" sometimes because I was so quiet but also because I got to see everything the guys were doing. I always laughed and made certain they knew I liked them and conveyed shyness. But the truth is, I was nervous all the time. At the end of each day, I wondered how long this wonderful new career would last. Alcohol calmed those nerves, but only for a few hours.

The project in Caddo Lake was ending soon. One morning I listened in on a conference call with upper management while they assessed the financial numbers. I loved taking part in any of the conversations with people in higher positions. I took tons of notes. As soon as I got home, after pouring myself a drink, I looked up important terms and anacronyms. I had to learn the jargon if I was going to catch up to everyone. I studied many of the land surveyor terms, like AMS (above mean sea level) and AMT (above mean terrain).

By the end of the conversation over the finances, they seemed pleased with Beau.

"You finished a month before the projected completion date, Beau. I don't know how you did it, but we are impressed," Spencer said.

Spencer was working in the corporate office as a project manager at the time. After a few more successful jobs like this last one, he would likely move up the chain as the new operations manager.

"Don't tell me you are impressed, Spencer," Beau said with a smug tone. "Show me you are impressed. My Christmas bonus better be big this year, pal."

"Your bonus will be what it will be, but I think you'll be pleased," Spencer said.

Beau looked at me to make sure I was listening and winked. Then everyone hung up.

"Let's celebrate!" Beau grabbed his jacket. "Pour us some drinks for the road, and let's hit the Horseshoe Casino."

"Wait a second. What happens now?" I asked, confused about why he was excited for the project to be completed a month before schedule. For me, the money train had come to a speedy end. *It had all been too good to be true*, I thought.

"What do you mean, what happens now? Weren't you listening? We celebrate!"

"No, I mean, what happens with work? Is it over? Do I need to go back to bartending?" I asked with my head down.

"You will never have to bartend again as long as you know me." Beau lifted up my chin until my light hazel eyes met his.

Why did I get goose bumps when he touched me? The sensation thrilled me and terrified me. Everyone finds themselves in reckless relationships sometimes. But getting involved with a coworker, especially my boss, was forbidden fruit—not to mention dumb and dangerous.

"Don't fret. There's another project kicking off at the end of next week in West Virginia. I was waiting to see how you did on this project before I mentioned it to you. But I have kept my eye on you—sometimes two—over the last few months. You have some more learning and maybe even a little growing up to do, but if you stick with me, I'll polish you up nicely."

Polish me up? Sheesh! Who did this guy think he was? "So does this mean I get to work the next project in West Virginia?"

"Yes, that's exactly what that means. This next project will be the last one before we shut down before Thanksgiving. Start saving your money now. The company will take on a couple of small jobs a few weeks before Christmas, and we won't return to work until just past Valentine's Day. It probably won't make sense now, but later you'll understand why we do this."

I never had a savings account. And I certainly never had someone telling me to save my money. But I clung to every word he said. I trusted him deeply. I was grateful for him and this opportunity. At the time I would have done anything Beau asked me to do, and I think he knew that too. He chose me to work for him because I would be loyal to him, and I would always have to follow his lead. It's much easier to manipulate a young, bright-eyed girl with hope. If he had hired a man, especially a man with knowledge of the industry, he wouldn't have had the amount of control he had over me. I had the alpha leader of the wolf pack by the tail and decided to hold on tight.

"Okay, let's celebrate!" I mixed up the best old-fashioneds, inspired by my favorite bartender in Louisiana, Scarlett. I made them with whiskey, orange, cherries, simple syrup, and a dash of bitters, with a twist for garnish. He loved them and drank them faster than I could garnish them.

The next week flew by. But by Friday afternoon, Beau had convinced me to trade in my Bronco for a roomier, more professional work vehicle. He promised to meet me at the dealership. I got there first. When I toured the lot, I fell in love with a blacked-out Cadillac Escalade. Me, in a Cadillac? Part of me was laughing at the ridiculousness of it all. Then I thought, *Why not me?*

The loan officer frowned at my work history. "You make plenty of money, but you have only been with your current employer for six months."

"Are you saying she needs a cosigner?" Beau asked, walking into the room. "This pretty thing is irreplaceable for me and the company."

When they shook hands, Beau gave him a look that it would be best if he disregarded my thin work history.

"No, she has the credit and the income. Just get me a letter stating she's contracted with the company for the next five years, and I'll get it past the bank. Let me go clear the path with my manager."

Helping me was another reason I believed he was truly separated. What kind of married man would suggest he could cosign for another woman's vehicle?

"Look at you," Beau said, sitting next to me. "You have good credit. I'm impressed."

Another compliment that was also demeaning. I'd lost track of how many times he made me feel special, then later feel like a fool after I thought about it. More red flags ignored. An hour later, I drove off the lot in my brand-new Cadillac Escalade and never felt more sophisticated in my life. I think that's another difference between men and women. For the most part, adult men don't try to be sophisticated. They are or they aren't. But women compete over looks and status.

When I pulled up to the hotel closest to the new gig in Summersville, my car still smelled brand new, despite the numerous fast-food bags on the floorboard. Throughout the thirteen-hour drive from Caddo Lake to West Virginia, I romanticized about Beau wanting me to have a perk for a job well done. It was a sweet gesture and had me smiling and singing the whole way. I was but a foolhardy young woman. I wish I could go back in time and pull off the blinders that were over my eyes. Buying the expensive car was just another ploy to keep me loyal and dependent on Beau and my new income.

After getting somewhat settled in the hotel, Beau met me in the parking lot. He was more than enthusiastic. I'd been around him enough to know when he was genuinely excited. And he was energized by this new project. It meant there was a whole lot of money at stake.

"This is where the jobsite will be," Beau said, showing me the layout of the site. "Save this location on your GPS and send the coordinates to all the guys. And I'll have them put your office here."

He pointed to one spot.

I didn't really care about where my office would be set up. My attention had drifted to the cool, crisp breeze that sent yellow-and-red leaves through the air. With the beautiful sunset in the background, Summersville was like a scene from a movie.

"Look at that view! It's breathtaking," I said, ignoring the details of the jobsite. "Too bad I don't have a window in my office. A girl could get used to seeing this every day."

When I arrived at the new office the next morning, the sun was not up yet. But I wasn't the first one there. I could hear loud saws and a generator running before I went inside. I closed the doors and walked over to Beau's desk.

"What's going on here?" I asked, staring at the two men working quickly to renovate one of the walls.

"They're cutting a hole in that wall and building you a window," he said with a smirk and a nod.

I couldn't believe he had listened to what I had said the night before.

"Thanks," I said with an air of nonchalance. I guarded my emotions in general, but more so around Beau. I still couldn't read him. Did he make the window as an act of kindness? Or was it another control measure so that he could see what I was doing? As much as I tried not to seem impressed, I was. And I think he saw right through my facade.

The next night we dined and drank at a local bar with some of the crew. I was in a wreck of a mood. Scarlett called me to chat before I had left the hotel. Besides being a bartender at my favorite bar in Shreveport, she also happened to be a great friend of mine over the years. She informed me the one and only *real* boyfriend I had growing up, Nathan, had been hitting on her at the bar. Then the group of friends had all gone out afterward, and he trashed me to everyone in earshot. I can't say why it bothered me so much. What did it matter? I had been away from the hometown crap for a long time. It was likely the abandonment issue rearing its ugly head. Sadly, my reaction was to throw back one too many shots that night.

"He didn't deserve me," I said, slurring a good portion of my words. I had trouble getting the straw of the margarita into my mouth, which caused some laughter. "He's a loser!" As I tried to control my hiccups, more laughter ensued.

"Okay, little miss. I think you've had enough. I can't let you drive that fancy new car of yours home in your condition. You're riding with me." It was Beau's voice, but my drinking had blurred my vision.

The next morning a harsh beam of sunlight woke me up. My head was pounding while I struggled to focus my vision. Then I noticed the arm around my waist. I sat up with alarm to see that Beau had shared the bed with me. Or rather, I had shared the bed with him. We were in his hotel room.

When I realized my clothes and his clothes were still on, the biggest wave of relief went through me. "Thank God," I said. I wondered if we had only cuddled, trying to replay the night's events in my mind.

Beau woke up and gave me a soft smile. "Morning, champ. How's your head?"

"Confused," I said, covering my breath.

"Relax, Sadie. We didn't . . . you know, if that's what you're wondering."

The second wave of relief washed over me. But I was also entertained by the fact that he wasn't comfortable using the word *sex* around me. I took it as a respectful and protective gesture, like he was watching what he said around a younger sister.

Then *that* thought bothered me. Did he think of me as a sister that needed protecting? Is that why he didn't try anything? Obviously, my thoughts were all over the place. I had to collect myself.

"I'm sorry I got so drunk last night," I said, offering a slight smile. "I hope I didn't make a fool out of myself."

"It was no problem. You were innocent."

We both purposefully ignored that we had woken up with his arms around me.

Neither of us mentioned the incident while working side by side over the next two weeks. Then Halloween came along. A few of the girls in the office invited everyone to a costume party, along with their significant others. I decided to go because there wasn't anything else to do, and there would be a lot to drink.

Before the fun really got started, Beau called me. He was hysterical. He explained that his best friend from high school had killed himself in his car. Beau was in uncontrollable tears. And I could hear how helpless he was through the phone.

"Come over," I said. It was out of my mouth before I could regret it.

"Where? I'm not going to that party."

"My hotel room. Just meet me there. I'll leave the party now."

"Okay, I'm heading out now," he said in a shaky voice. "And Sadie. Thanks for being a good friend." Then he hung up.

When he pulled into the parking lot, he was a drunken

blubbering mess. His arm was red and bloody from a tattoo he had clearly gotten earlier in the night. If it was his friend's name, no one would ever be able to read it.

I walked him to my room. Fortunately, it was on the first floor.

"Are you okay?" I asked, trying to be sensitive. Sensitivity did not come naturally to me. I grew up in a house where affection was nonexistent. I was in uncharted waters.

He let out a deep sigh. "I'll never be able to forgive myself. I ignored all his calls. He reached out to me five times last month. I kept telling him I was too busy to chat." He wiped his eyes. "I'm such a shit friend," he said, repeating it through his tears.

I said nothing else. I wrapped my arms around him, and I hugged him tight. To no one's surprise, the hug turned into a kiss. The strong taste of bourbon filled my lungs. And I wondered if he was going to remember this tomorrow.

"These things happen." I wiped a tear from his cheek. "People lose touch all the time. Try to remember the good times. You weren't a bad friend. Don't beat yourself up."

He said nothing, never losing eye contact with me. I just stood there, dressed in a skimpy ghost costume as he cried.

It's never funny when a grown man cries, so I took in the moment. I was a bit torn, trying to figure out why he chose to call me that night. Part of me was thankful he did.

"You look ridiculous, by the way," Beau said, wiping away the last of the tears.

"That's the whole point." I twirled around, giving him the full view.

"Ridiculously sexy too." He smiled again.

"You think so?" I said as if fishing for compliments.

He kissed me again, and I didn't pull away.

We spent the rest of the night talking and flirting while listening to sad songs. I poured us drink after drink. Then the sun turned the sky pink before poking its head over the fence.

"Would you like to dance with me?" he asked.

"Sure," I said with a flirty smile. My accent flooded back as the excessive alcohol broke the dam. "But ya know what they say if ya go dancin' with a ghost."

We spun around the room while the sun came up, and for a moment the world stood still.

I guess everyone is just a friend I no longer speak to.
My nails scratch the wall.
I needed to make sure I was not a ghost.
I notice a crack in the window, and I long to be a bird.
I wanted to be rescued.
But I didn't believe in fairy tales.

CHAPTER EIGHT
Provoking the Wolf

THE WINTER HOLIDAYS FLEW BY AS USUAL. I stayed in Summersville for most of it. But we had a few more weeks before the next project in the southeast corner of Iowa, so I took a quick trip back to see Maw-maw. It wasn't a gushy or huggy reunion, but we were both happy to see each other's faces while we talked. I didn't visit with any friends. I didn't want to be in Shreveport for long. I had a new, promising life. And being home had a way of stirring up bad feelings all around.

The work crew wondered why I chose to stay on the jobsites when the projects were over rather than going home. I didn't have a home at that point. And we were always on the move. It was hotel after hotel and short-term corporate housing on the longer projects. I didn't even have a permanent apartment. I went wherever the job took me. I had just enough belongings to fill up my car, and that was it. Not having roots anywhere prompted a loneliness if I thought about it too much. Yet I felt liberated at the same time. I had escaped the routine ruts of Shreveport.

As luck would have it—bad luck, that is—I ran into my ex in the parking lot of Walmart on my way out of town. I was getting into my SUV, when I heard someone calling my name.

"Is that you, Sadie?"

There he was. Nathan, the liar and cheater, the one who sullied my reputation in front of everyone in town.

"Who's asking?" I said coldly.

"There's my funny girl," Nathan said as he approached.

"I'm not your girl anymore." If I was capable of spitting venom, I would have.

He smiled anyway. "But you are still funny. How are you? I barely recognized you. New wheels? You look really good, Sadie."

He didn't *really* know me back when we dated, and he sure as hell didn't know me now. "Yeah, I got a new job, and I needed something bigger and better on gas."

"Abby told me about your new job. I'm so proud of you. And I'm really happy for you too. I want to apologize for everything. I'm so sorry I hurt you. I'm sorry for all the things I said about you. I'd been drinking, and I heard you were having fun at casinos, living it up with some handsome guy. I guess I acted jealous. That's not an excuse at all though. I shouldn't have let a bruised ego get the best of me."

"That guy is my boss," I said. "And you had no right to make up fake rumors about me to try and make yourself seem like the victim."

"I know that, Bugs," Nathan said.

He called me his *little bug*. It was our thing. One night he was trying to text *I love you big* and spell-check changed it to *bug*. I thought he meant to call me bug, so I replied *I love you too, big bug*. Silly, but it stuck.

"Look, Sadie. I'm truly sorry. Would it be possible to have your new number? I want to stay friends with you. I do miss you, and I'm so proud of you."

I'd be bold-faced lying if I said it didn't feel good to rub my new life in his face. It made me smile inside when he saw me in my new car, wearing new clothes. I wasn't as weak as I was when we had dated, and it showed. I handed him my business card. "Sure, we can be friends. I'm leaving town tomorrow for a few months. Maybe we can catch up when I get back."

He messaged me as soon as I drove off. "Here is my number, Little Bug. Save it."

Maybe because I was young and dumb, or maybe I could sense some jealous potential in Beau, but I decided to save him in my phone as Catherine. She was another friend I had known since grade school. I talked about her just often enough so Beau wouldn't suspect anything if he looked at my phone. And it wasn't that I had anything to hide. I avoided drama wherever I could, and I had no idea where I stood with Beau. Another flag? You bet, and I ignored it along with all the others.

As we prepared to kick off the next project in Iowa, I worried things with Beau would go back to the way they started. Could we really keep this going in front of our colleagues without receiving any kind of flack? I played with the white-gold tennis bracelet on my wrist. Beau had bought it for me at Christmas. I liked to stare at the three small diamonds sparkling in the center, and I never wanted to take it off. The only reason I knew he spent more than two grand on it was because he left the price tag on it. He probably did that on purpose, but it was the most expensive piece of jewelry

I ever owned. And I cherished it.

Later that week, Beau and I went sightseeing. The winding roads brought us through the gorgeous emerald hillsides and pristine lakes. There were fresh springs and spacious farmland to stop and wander through if we were inclined. That's when I realized all our assignments were near small towns surrounded by a lot of beautiful land. I wondered why.

Beau and I were drinking my famous old-fashioneds at noon while working. When we ran out of oranges and cherries, we took a ride to a local mart that had a gas station attached.

"I'll run in and grab what we need," I said, leaving my work phone behind.

While I was inside, my phone had buzzed several times. I found out as soon as I got back in the car.

"Your phone is blowing up," Beau said with furrowed eyebrows.

"Okay," I said, taking a sip from my drink before it got too warm.

"Aren't you going to check it to see if it's work calling or family?"

I suspected he already knew who it was by the way he acted, but I had a password on my phone, so I couldn't be certain. I unlocked my phone. *Catherine* was texting me.

"It's just my friend Catherine," I said, feeling uneasy. "I'll text her later."

"Are you sure that's who was texting you?" he asked in an accusatory tone.

The last of the red flags flew by in a gust of angry wind.

"Yes, I'm sure," I said, looking him in the eye. And I tried to figure out how he could've gotten my phone's passcode.

"Wrong answer!" With no warning, Beau grabbed my hair and slammed my face into the center console.

Before I could even register what had happened, I tasted blood. I picked my head up and spit the blood out of my mouth. I started to cry, still in utter shock at what had just happened.

Beau drove faster and screamed with rage. "Since when does Catherine call you *Bug*? I'll bet you don't remember telling me at the bar the other night that your ex calls you that! And you probably can't remember a damn thing! Can you? You're a dumb, fucking drunk slut!"

I cried louder, still unable to say anything. There was nothing to say, if I could. I had lied. He caught me. He gave me the chance to tell the truth, and I chose to lie.

Beau spun the tires and spit the stones in the parking lot of the hotel where his truck was parked. Then he grabbed the emergency brake. The SUV did a fishtail, and we slid to a stop.

Everything had happened so fast, and I tried to catch my breath. Once the vehicle came to a stop, I looked at him with a mouthful of blood. "I'm sorry," I whispered.

"Oh, you're fucking sorry now?" He grabbed me by my ponytail. He pulled my face into his face. "And what exactly are you sorry for? Being a whore or for trying to make me look like a fucking clown?" Beau spit in my face. His breath was hot and foul, and his eyes were feral, like a rabid wolf. "No one makes me look like a clown!" Before he released my hair from his grip, he pushed my head one last time into the console, rubbing it on the leather while smearing the blood onto my face. "You are so done, you dumb bitch."

I sat there and sobbed for several minutes, then he jumped out of my car and stormed off to his truck. He drove away, kicking rocks into the air from his oversized tires on his jacked-up Dodge Ram.

For an hour, maybe longer, I sat in my SUV with blood dripping from my face and hands. Shaking with fear, my brain tried to replay everything a dozen times, and I still couldn't grasp it all. What had just happened to me? I wiped my mouth and stared at myself in my visor mirror.

In moments like that, it's sometimes odd who you reach out to for help. I called Renee, the only person I knew in the area at the time. She and I grew up together, until she moved away to go to college. Ironically, she lived close to the area we were working in. I had called her while I was first driving to the new site so we could catch up. Renee and her husband had taken Beau and I out on their boat a few weekends. She seemed to like him, from what I could tell. But this call to her was a cry for help. I told her some of what had happened and asked if I could stay the night with her. Without a doubt, I was scared, more so than any time in my life.

When I got there, she hugged me. "Sadie, tell me what happened."

I couldn't speak. I let my wounds do the talking. All I kept thinking was that I'd lost my job. My brain tried to cope with the severe trauma by focusing on the mundane. How was I going to afford my new car and my new debts? I would need to work at three different bars to make the same amount of money. I'm not sure *humiliated* was the right word. I felt like a failure. I turned my phone off, then drank the rest of the whiskey I had in the center console, the console covered in my own dried blood.

I woke up before the sun did the next morning, empty and scared. I thought about my job and how upset Beau had gotten. Did he remember hitting me? Maybe he had gotten more drunk than either of us realized. I still have no idea why I conjured up excuses for him in that moment. A pattern I would later repeat. Instead of driving away as far as I could from a boss who had just brutalized me or calling the police, I brainstormed how I could fix the situation. My psyche had plunged face-first into a dark well. My self-esteem, cockiness, confidence—gone. In just a few moments of violent trauma, my whole world had been cast to the wind.

I wrote Renee a thank-you note and sneaked out before she woke up. Then I drove straight to where Beau was staying. I felt my heart sink to my feet as I knocked. Was he still mad at me? Would he hit me again? Beau opened the door and looked at me. My hazel eyes were puffy and bloodshot from crying all night. My swollen, bruised face told the tale of having been smashed on my SUVs center console.

"I'm sorry," I said, looking up at Beau. "Please talk to me." I couldn't tell if it was defeat in my voice or desperation—probably both.

"Are you okay, Sadie? I've been worried, and I tried calling you last night. You weren't in any condition to drive. Where did you go?"

"Renee's place—I swear!" I relaxed ever so slightly when I thought he believed me. Pack leaders set painful boundaries. And there was no chance I'd be stupid enough to lie to him again.

"I take it you told her your side of the story and made her believe I'm a shitty person?"

Even in such a fragile moment between us, Beau was more concerned with his reputation and what he might have to say at the office than the dried blood on my teeth.

"No, I didn't tell her anything," I said with a reassuring glance.

I could only hold my gaze to his eyes for a second. "I told her I got into a drunken bar fight with another girl. She believed me."

He seemed relieved by that response. "Look, Sadie, I'm sorry, okay? I don't know why I reacted so harshly. I let the drink get the best of me. I was drunk and jealous. I don't like it when people try to make a fool out of me. It goes back to my childhood."

I pleaded as if I was the one who should apologize to him. "It will never happen again!"

There was an awkward silence as I stood in the open doorway.

"I guess I'm fired," I muttered with my head down. "I'll pack my things and head home today."

"You're not fired," Beau said, annoyed with me for worrying about my job. "Your job is safe for now. I need you on the site. We've a lot more work to do. Let's be civil, and we can part ways on the next project."

He knew the incident wouldn't look good to human resources, and I didn't know at the time about employee rights in the workplace. He probably knew I was clueless and never told me about the laws set in place made to protect people like me. If I had been more knowledgeable, I could've been protected. Instead, I was disposable. My fate lay in Beau's hands from then on.

Any rational woman would have left and reported him to the police. That's what anyone with wisdom would say. Most women wouldn't have come back that morning. Parts of me were broken before I met Beau because of my childhood, but now everything I thought I was and who I thought I could be had been shattered. To move on, I had to tell myself lies.

By allowing me to keep my job, Beau made me feel like I owed him. The least I could do was pretend that none of this happened.

Besides, he was drunk, and he'd never do anything like that if he was sober. He was in a fit of rage. Love makes you crazy sometimes. I definitely heard that expression before. It didn't matter we were never in love. Every lie was an excuse, a defense mechanism, to make him seem better than he was. Telling myself that I would never see the feral rage again made me justify his behavior. This was easier to do during the times he was so blacked out and didn't remember hitting me. It was survival mode in the pack, or so I thought.

I had the remainder of the current project to convince him to let me go on the next one, or I'd have to find a new job or multiple jobs to just afford my new car. I had to move fast. When I look back, I know my brain needed a task to put some distance between my terrible mistake and to get back in favor with Beau. That next week I pounced on any chance to compliment him and worked harder than I ever had before. I had to be flawless. I couldn't afford one mistake.

I acted more ladylike, the way he said women were supposed to behave before they got the right to vote. I toned down my sassy attitude. I spoke the way he said women were supposed to speak before they got the right to open their own checking accounts. Whether I knew it or not, I had become submissive to Beau.

He enjoyed my compliments. And he fished for more. He smiled when I was submissive. And I felt good whenever I made him proud. Underneath it all was the beginning of a living hell for me. The moment I didn't run, I was trapped. I let him know he was allowed to hit me without a single repercussion. I'd lost control over everything. Beau owned me.

I tried to imagine a life outside my reality.
Where would I go? The world is my oyster.
I was forced to think about forgiveness.
Not for you but forgiveness within myself.
Maybe I would go out tomorrow.
For now, I will close the blinds because I have no use for the sun.

CHAPTER NINE
Fairy Tales

After Iowa, Salt Lake City was the next gig. Beau and I both seemed to be in a good headspace. We were back together, so to speak, and we were still impressing everyone at work. He oversaw the projects, while I reported back to upper management. Together we designed new forms and new ways to track jobsite information. Everyone in the office raved about us. We were quite the duo.

Hard to believe it had only been a month since the hurricane of a fight. In true hurricane fashion, it destroyed everything around us. The trust was gone, replaced with suspicion. Respect was gone, replaced with fear. Any love that might have been brewing was long gone. There was now just a codependency. I kept him happy, and I kept my job.

As the weeks went by, we still had a desire to be close to one another. I didn't want him, but I'd be damned if someone else could have him. I think he felt the same way about me. But I wasn't sure whether it was him I was afraid of losing, or if I was terrified of who I was without him. When he started staying away from me for weeks at a time, suspicions grew like weeds in my mind.

It wasn't long before I discovered he had been staying with his wife during these stints. I also learned he was never separated from her. He was full-blown married. To add further pain to my splintered self-esteem, Caroline was beautiful. About the same time she found out about me, I found an old photo ID of hers in his truck.

Imagine my shock when she texted me. "I know about you, home-wrecker."

Anger, shame, the desire to confront her and him, all mixed in my head as I drank. When I saw Beau again, I was livid. Wisdom? Red flags? No, those were gone forever. And I'd drunk enough to not really care if I lost my job or not. I wanted to fight about the situation until he gave me some answers.

I showed Beau the text and demanded to know what was going on. "No more lies! Just be straight up with me. Are you still married?"

When I lied about texting "Catherine," I was punched in the mouth. But I was supposed to just overlook it when he lied about an entire marriage.

"I told you it was complicated," Beau said as if I was overdramatizing a tiny technicality. "I never lied to you."

I was furious and flung my hands in the air. "Complicated? Does that mean you two are separated? Does that mean you're happy? I'm confused as to what your definition of *complicated* is at this point."

His voice remained steady, like he could care less that I was upset. "It's harder to leave when kids are involved, Sadie. You can bet all you own that she and I are not happy, and I am working toward my divorce."

"Then why is she texting me and calling me a *home-wrecker*? Explain that one to me!"

"I told you we got together in high school, and I got her pregnant. She has never worked a day in her life, and she didn't finish high school. She relies on me for money. Caroline thinks you are going to mess with her piggy bank. She doesn't want me any more than I want her. But because of our marriage, she gets access to most of my money and benefits. And she knows about you because I told her. Don't pay her any mind. She thinks because I'm with you, I'll take away her lifestyle. She could give two craps about me. And that's why I called her a dumb bitch that night at the casino. She has bipolar disorder, and she overacts in waves."

It was one heck of a story. And being the gullible girl I was, I believed all of it because it made things easier for me. Later, when all the dust settled, I learned she never had bipolar disorder.

Beau had an answer for everything, and he spoke with such conviction. There were times in the office when he would tell a lie to someone, and I knew it. He was smooth in that way. He never had to stop and think of an answer. Lying came easily for him, as if it were his second language.

Because of my mental state, it was better just to believe the pretty lies.

"What do you say we go to Dallas for the weekend? The 'Boys are playing a home game, and I want to take you. Invite Abby, and I'll pay for the entire trip." Just like that, the topic was off his wife, Caroline, and on to pro football. If I backtracked to the previous subject, there might be retribution. So I played along.

"Abby is the biggest football fan, but she hates the Cowboys," I said with a finger on my chin. "But we could still have fun hanging out. She doesn't get to go on many vacations."

"Where is she again?"

"She lives in Lafayette now."

"Okay, let's invite her. Set it up. We'll fly her up and get a couple of rooms at a five-star hotel in downtown Dallas. How does that sound?"

"Sounds good to me," I said, trying to hide my excitement.

That's how he did it. Beau had a knack for taking the heat off him. If his smooth talk didn't work, he bought his way out. I wondered, then, how he had so much money. I understood his salary afforded him a lot. But he wasn't a millionaire. When I added Caroline's drain on his resources with the money he used to keep his entire family living comfortably, there shouldn't have been much left over. Regardless of my suspicions, I didn't question him on it.

The sad truth was that I enjoyed living the lifestyle Beau provided. Though twisted and destructive, I felt like I earned it because of the violence and walking on eggshells. We went to several Cowboys games that year. And we were always jet-setting somewhere expensive. If a contract finished early, or there was a break due to the weather, we traveled to the finest resorts. We ate kingly meals. A few times, we didn't even pack our bags. Beau bought us all new clothes when we arrived. Whenever Abby came along, I enjoyed sharing with her some of the *good life.*

Did I know back then Beau was manipulating me instead of being genuinely nice? I did deep down, but when the rational protests crawled to the surface, I smacked them back into the dark.

After the first brutal blowup with Beau, I got frugal with my money. The new fear was any given day could be my last with the company. I decided to be prepared for the possibility of going back to bartending. Even though I was only twenty-three, I had just put down 3 percent on a brand-new home in Oklahoma. I was the youngest homeowner out of all my friends.

My home was beautiful. Beau helped me pick it out, of course. It made sense to me to get a house near Thackerville. I knew the area, and it was centrally located around all the jobs we got assigned to. The real estate and taxes were incredibly low in Love County, and I had made some real friendships there. It was a dream home to me. And Beau liked the notion of having a home there with me, and we were only a few hours' drive to the Dallas games.

The location was also convenient for Beau because my house was within driving distance to Caroline's house. I referred to it that way on purpose. Beau was married and would likely stay that way for a long time. But it made things easier on my already tortured soul by saying she had her house while I had mine. I viewed my house like a fairy-tale castle, and Beau lived with me.

We stayed there only when it was football season, and there were a few home games in a row. Beau was a devoted Dallas Cowboys fan. I've never met anyone else whose mood could so drastically hinge on whether a sports team won or not. When they did win, he would be on cloud nine and would buy a round of shots for every person in the bar. But when the Cowboys lost, no one had fun. Beau was mean and cruel with his words. He would pout and drag his feet the rest of the day like a toddler who couldn't control his temper tantrums. As my luck would have it, the Cowboys were in a funk for years while I was with him. A downturn in their glorious history led to added anxiety for me.

It wasn't always football games that put Beau in a foul mood. He had a sharp tongue and bared his teeth when he felt like it. He had a way of cutting someone down with his words. Not just me but anyone. It's almost as if he studied a person before he met them so he could find out exactly what made them tick. He would find out the things in life they feared the most—the things that haunted them and kept them up at night. Those were the fuel for his fire to use against them.

I never understood that part about Beau. And given my predicament, I rationalized what caused his violent behavior, believing it had nothing to do with who he really was. Had he been hurt and abused as a child? What left him so cold? I asked myself those questions often. He had this aura of being beautifully broken. He was the type of man you could be vulnerable with while he was sober, only to regret it when he was drunk. But Beau wasn't always a nasty drunk. He was like the weather. If something upset him, he was a raging storm. We drank every day for as long as I knew him. Most of the time, we had fun.

He and I had that bond, drinking every day. It was destructive in multiple ways, yet it was still a connection between us. When you find yourself in a dark hole, you grasp anything you can to keep from falling down farther. I clung to alcohol like a safety raft. As long as I had it within my reach, there was no way I could drown in my emotions.

Beau would be fine to hang out with until he wasn't. There was a turning point where if he had just one sip too many his eyes glossed over, and he was soulless. At that point he did not care who he hurt—mentally, physically, financially, or emotionally. Beau loved to fight. He often bragged about his days growing up in the ghetto as a young boy. And he blamed being in and out of jail as a teenager and a young adult on his harsh upbringing. Petty theft and fighting had been the main reasons.

One day, in the office, someone who rarely spoke to me whispered a bit of Beau's history. Those who knew him in his formative years guessed he'd wind up a criminal mastermind by the time he was eighteen. I added that nugget to the countless stories I heard about Beau over the years, though most were from him. Like the first day he entered my bar, I still couldn't figure out which parts of his life were true and which parts were lies.

The tricky thing about lying is keeping it straight over a long period of time. And if you repeat it enough, you believe it yourself. That went for me too. I had been lying to myself and all those who knew some of the ugly happenings in my world. I never let anyone know it, not even Maw-maw.

I made excuses for Beau's behavior like a mother defending her rotten son. I was losing track of which parts of our relationship were lies, and I think everyone around me suspected that. I started lying on social media as well. I only posted photos of my luxurious lifestyle. I needed to make sure no one suspected I was living a double life with a married man. Everyone got to see the great parts of our relationship, and I left the unpleasant bits out.

I let the world believe what they wanted. This is what made it so difficult later, trying to convince everyone I had truly been abused. In hindsight, our relationship was a farce, no matter how much I painted it as a fairy tale.

The truth was evident.
The alcohol helped feed my true addiction—that was you.
So I did the only thing I knew to do.
I removed the knife from my back,
and I kept it in a safe place in the rare chance that you may come back one day asking for it.
If I hadn't kept it safe for you,
what kind of person would I be?

CHAPTER TEN
Acquiescence at the Bottom

THERE'S SOMETHING ABOUT FOOTBALL SEASON in the South. It's almost like a religion. And each time we went home to Thackerville or flew straight to Dallas for a game, Beau spent ten grand like it was nothing. There was no bottom to his endless wallet.

Every weekend he and I did something extravagant, and I couldn't understand where all the money was coming from. Beau was a puzzle to me on every level. And my mind tried to put the pieces together, but there were always some missing.

I told myself not to give up on him. His ugly behavior couldn't be his fault. I needed to try harder to understand him better, secretly hoping to make him whole again. If I could fix the parts in him that were broken, he would finally see all the pain he was causing me, and he would apologize in a grand way. These are the kind of things victims of verbal and physical abuse tell themselves. No one wants to admit they picked a rotten apple—someone cruel or downright evil. The ego is always trying to be right, no matter how hard it is to twist the truth in your mind.

If I could take away Beau's pain, I figured I could rid myself of my troubles. But he was such a complex creature. I was always one step behind. He'd have the entire weekend all planned out beforehand. He left little of the decision-making to me.

"Pack a bag. We are flying out this weekend. The 'Boys are playing the Deadskins. And I got us front-row seats at midfield. We are staying at the Joule. After that, we are meeting some clients tonight, so pack your boots." Beau thought a man could be described by the type of boots he wore. Usually, he wore camel-colored boots made from exotic animals—wearing shoes made from dead animals was a bit morbid, if you ask me. But he couldn't help but notice everyone's boots and make his own assumptions based on that alone.

"Look at that guy. He's such a pussy. Wearing cheap ostrich boots like that—you can tell he's never worked a day in his life." I heard that rant more than once when we were at bars. And he always said those things about good-looking men or well-dressed men. Beau was as insecure and damaged as I was, and his bravado was his shield. I couldn't stop him from judging another man based on his appearance, so I'd just agree with him to make things easier. And Beau wanted me to agree with him out loud for reassurance.

I once made the mistake of disagreeing with him about someone who had walked past us. "I like his boots, and he seems charming," I said. I never heard the end of it.

"You just want to fuck him, you dumb bitch." That's all it took. To deviate from his point of view and the code of conduct he set out for me meant instant wrath.

Never again, I told myself. Never again will I disagree with him when he acted like that. It wasn't enough to agree with him that the other guy looked silly. It was required that I point out Beau's strengths. I had to compare him to other men, then shower him with compliments over his good looks and intelligence. I had to lie a lot. But I would never dare tell him I thought another man was attractive, even if it was painfully obvious.

Beau always found something wrong with other men's appearance, like it was a nervous tick. I remember him making fun of Chris Hemsworth one day. How can you say he is ugly and keep a straight face? I just had to bite my tongue and fabricate a flaw like his eyes were too close together. It became mentally exhausting having to think of the right response every time I spoke. I lived in fear with multiple layers. As crazy as it sounds, most days I would rather have been physically scolded than verbally.

Beau knew the vilest thing to say that would make me want to crawl out of my own skin and die. He never showed the ugliest side of himself when other people were around. Beau was too calculating and vain to allow that to happen.

If someone's comment or behavior triggered him at dinner, you'd never know Beau was upset until we were back in the hotel room. His anger slow cooked in his head, simmering until we were behind closed doors. Then all hell would break loose. And that's what terrified me the most. I always had to wonder what Beau's mindset was from one second to the next. And I had to make sure he knew I was paying attention, letting him know I was on his side no matter what.

When we arrived in Dallas, like we had so many times before, I prayed for the Cowboys to win. I could care less about professional football, but the outcome of the game would impact the weekend drastically. Staying at the Joule Hotel, we were able to walk everywhere and didn't have to worry about drinking and driving. We would start drinking at 7:00 a.m. on most days. Driving from my house in Thackerville wasn't an option for him. Beau preferred to party without any hassles.

Abby arrived in midafternoon. She was fun and beautiful. We'd become closer than ever over the last few years. She was more of a sister to me, so much so I called her son my nephew to everyone I met.

She wasn't afraid of voicing her opinions and kept her wits about her. And Abby didn't take crap from anyone. There was comfort knowing I never had to wonder what she was thinking when we were together. Naturally, when she was around me and Beau, I only showed her the parts of him she would approve of. Secretly, I hoped he would show his true colors around her. I had a fantasy that if she knew the truth, she'd help me leave.

Unfortunately for me, Beau kept his control unless we were alone. I always wondered if she ever saw past my smile or knew I was hiding something. I have never asked her. Being with Beau was like social media. I only showed people the highlight reel. I talked about our trips in a way no one could suspect anything. I showed off my shopping trophies and took pictures of our extravagant meals, never letting on how much I suffered to have those things. And I didn't dare tell anyone about his wife, Caroline, or his violent temper. I ignored them while tiptoeing on the eggshells, hoping they might go away. But they never did.

When Abby got out of the taxi, I was already waiting for her at the curb. She ran up and hugged me, her jet-black hair behind her ear. I hugged her back so tightly and wished I could tell her how desperately I needed that hug. We had similar eyes, body shape, and attitude. Wherever we went, we were accused of being sisters. We often played it up just for fun. She and I got good at making up all kinds of childhood stories—how we would get in trouble and what rebels we had been as kids.

"Ready for a drink?" I asked her.

Abby checked her watch as if there was an official time one should start drinking. Those social constructs were never a consideration in my world. "Sure, I'll have a glass of wine."

She wasn't a big drinker like Beau and me. Not many were. Abby liked to put back a few now and then, but she was a lightweight. Although she didn't have to drink much, Abby was a fun drunk. After a few beers, you might find her onstage, dancing and singing with the band. Or she would tease strangers for a kiss while wrapping a boa of feathers around their necks. She was divorced, worked too many hours per week, and didn't have much time for fun.

Our weekends in Dallas provided Abby with a chance to blow off steam and be whoever she wanted to be. Beau liked Abby, and that was important. If he decided he didn't like one of my friends, I was forbidden to speak to them. It was the main reason I lost a lot of friends while he and I were together.

Beau had a best friend who would meet up with us most of the time. He'd go to the games and almost all the vacations we took. Sawyer was a coastal Florida boy from the Panhandle. He was from Santa Rosa and had the accent to match. He ended sentences with a "shug," a short for *sugar* when addressing females.

Sawyer was also married. And I never understood his marriage either. He was like some character on a reality show. He had many girlfriends over the ten years I'd known him. And not just flings but girls he considered marrying. They knew about his wife, Alex, and he swore she knew about all of them. Their marriage was similar to Beau and Caroline's, as she was dependent upon Sawyer's income and resources. He said she was equally uneducated and had a pill addiction, so that made her hard to love. Anytime Beau and I were planning a getaway, he wanted Sawyer to come with us. So he'd suggest I bring one of my friends from back home. If they hit it off, then it would be a fun time. If not, the trip was spoiled.

If Sawyer had a falling-out with one of my friends, I was forbidden to communicate with them, let alone see them. Therefore, I made sure Beau knew Abby was off-limits. Sawyer was never allowed to hit on her.

Beau didn't have many friends outside the company. There were several friends who would often travel with us to nice places.

And because they all worked for the company, when the whole group got together, a $10,000 weekend turned into $30,000. They all waved their company credit cards in the air, swiping them for rooms, flights, tickets, expensive foods and drinks, limousines, and *entertainment*. They were shameless.

I wondered at the end of those extravagant weekends how the company had any money left over. One time they blew twenty grand on a bottle of Pappy Van Winkle. None of them batted an eye when they paid for the bar tabs. They either made a lot more money than I saw coming in or had some scheme going to milk the company dry. But I never asked. I did what they told me to do and kept my mouth shut.

One thing I thought odd was they never kept or turned in receipts. I assumed those would be needed by the accounting department. I didn't understand company policies at all. Although I observed a lot, I just went with the flow.

Weekends with Abby were never long enough. When we hugged goodbye, we told each other to be good. I told her I loved her and promised to schedule another outing soon. But I never told her how hard I cried when I watched her drive off to the airport. My heart knew it was more than loneliness.

My initial prayer went unanswered, as Dallas had lost that weekend. And when they lost, Beau became the worst sore sport in the world. He decided he wanted to drive out of the city and stay at my house that night.

"I'm never spending money on another game," he said as he sulked behind the wheel.

Beau drank hard liquor the entire way home, cussing and complaining about the shit calls by the referees and how poorly the team played. By then, I knew better than to do or say a thing that might make it worse when he was in one of his belligerent and irate moods.

All I tried to do the whole way home was to be a source of comfort. If we could just make it back to the house, I knew he would settle down a bit. But that night breathing too loud was a federal offense. Before we made it home, he'd already thrown my GPS, cell phone, and police scanner out of the window. He didn't care; he would just replace them all on the company dime. He continued to drink even after we got home. I drank to keep him company. At least, that's how I rationalized it to myself.

The hours blurred, and the next thing I knew, we were in the midst of a heated argument. I never knew what triggered it. There was a turning point in Beau's drunkenness that caused him to want to fight no matter what. And there was a turning point in my drunkenness that caused me to stop caring if I told him what I thought. A perfect combo for disaster.

I was brave and mouthy for only a few minutes before he made me regret it. Some people say the best thing to do when confronting a wild animal is to yell as loud as possible, then make yourself appear bigger. Don't back down, and never run. Those people had never met Beau drunk to the point of insanity. I can only guess I got tired of listening to him complain and cry over a stupid football game. I remember saying something like, "Just get over it already!"

He was acting like a toddler and had ruined my day. I didn't want it to carry over into the next morning. I had hoped he would just take that as an opportunity to leave rather than fight, but I wasn't that lucky.

Beau began belittling me like he usually did. But I pushed him to full fury when I started beating him to his own punch lines. After all, I heard them so many times in previous fights.

"I know—I'm so fat and ugly, right? I'm the dumbest bitch on the planet. I've never met a trashier woman in my life." I knew his tricks and pretended his words were just bluster. If I took away his hurtful words, he would be left without any ammo. He would either have to stop long enough to pass out or just leave.

Beau had other plans that night. He grabbed anything and everything he could reach and smashed it on the floor. He broke lamps, vases, picture frames, and gifts from family until there wasn't anything left to break. Except for me.

He cocked his arm back as if he was going to strike me, then paused before his fist hit my face. He showed his teeth and said,

"You would like that, wouldn't you?"

I was drunk, but I was still scared. I tried to run for the door. Beau was like a hungry wolf in the woods in that sense. There was no way he was going to let me out of his sight and give me the chance to summon some help.

"I'm not ever going back to jail," he said with a growl. Beau grabbed me by the shirt and twisted his fist up in order to get a good grip. He threw me to the floor. Drunk and stunned, I curled into a fetal position. He kicked my legs with his steel-toe boots with as much force as he could. He missed half the time, but it didn't matter. "This will teach you to run, you dumb bitch!"

When he was done kicking me, he dragged me into my bathroom, then forced me into the oversized bathtub. He turned the water on. I was fading in and out. Then he held my head under the cold water, grinning while I squirmed for air.

This is it, I thought to myself. This was how I would die—murdered in my own tub. And I wondered if I was the first woman to die by his devilry. He threatened me many times over the years that he knew enough places to bury me in a deep hole, where even bloodhounds had no chance of sniffing me out.

While drowning, I managed to get my head and arms out of the shirt he'd been holding so tight. I was only in my underwear, but I slipped free from his grip. I stood up and took off. How I managed to run and not slip on the wet tile, I'll never know. God helped me at that exact moment, for sure.

I whipped open the door and ran outside, with my bare body exposed. I made it across the street to a house that still had one light on. I didn't dare look back. The owner of the house was an older man with a brown beard. Shock registered on his face, seeing me half naked, shivering, and soaking wet. I wailed hysterically.

He ushered me into his home. "Get a towel or a sheet!" His startled wife scurried down a hallway. I still remember the kind warmth of the blanket that matched her voice. I was blacking in and out when she sat me down. Her husband clicked the bullets into his pistol and asked me to tell them what had happened.

I did. They called 911. He was a retired police officer and assured me I was safe. Within minutes, the police arrived at his home and not mine. One officer took my statement, and another officer walked over to my house with my neighbor. They wanted to locate Beau and hear his side of the horror story or confirm mine. Beau was nowhere to be found. But there was broken glass and plaster everywhere from all the items he broke. There was a trail of water from the bathroom to the front door, and my clothes were still sitting in the bathtub.

"Her story matches up," the younger officer said to his superior.

I remember being unable to blink while wondering if they thought anyone could make up a story like that and have the body marks to prove it. After they took my full statement, they had to take photos of the cuts and scratches on my body, and the deep bruise developing on my thigh. At this point the bruise was the size of a watermelon, but in a few days it would cover my entire thigh down to almost my knee. The cops explained they were going to keep an eye on my house for the rest of the night in the event Beau came back. They told me once they caught him it was more than likely he'd be arrested, if I decided to press charges.

Beau never came back to my house that night, and I did not sleep a wink. The next day I heard from Sawyer before midday. After he told me where Beau was staying, I drove over there. I knocked on the door, and he let me in. He was calmer than I thought he would be.

He didn't have to say anything, and neither did I.

I forgave him like I had before. No, it wasn't forgiveness. Acquiescence is more accurate. I crawled into the bed and laid down next to him.

He wrapped his arms around me. "I'm sorry, baby," he whispered as he started to cry.

As always, I couldn't be sure if his tears were real, or if he was putting on a show just to manipulate me. Either way, I never pressed charges on him. I was too broken and confused. Any power or control I might've had at my disposal shrunk away with the shame and guilt. My mind searched for the safest person to blame and condemn.

Maybe I shouldn't have called the cops. Had I overreacted? This is all my fault. I should have just let him sulk. I would be upset, too, if I spent that much money and my team lost. I should be thankful he invited me. We were both drunk. I'm lucky he invited me.

I prayed Beau would let me keep my job. I'd reached the bottom, and my only focus was convincing him that I was sorry too. I didn't even clean up the disaster in my home. We both just left town and went back to work on the road. It wasn't until I came home for Thanksgiving that I had to face the mess in my house.

I crumbled into a million pieces,
until those pieces turned into dust.
There was officially nothing left of me.
I was equal parts dust and silence.

CHAPTER ELEVEN
Eye for an Eye

I HAVE ALWAYS LOVED CALIFORNIA. When I was a kid, I dreamed of sticking my toes in the sand with the Pacific Ocean washing over them. When I ran away from home, that was the first thing I did. So you can imagine how much my spirits were lifted when I found out our next project with the company was just outside San Diego.

Whenever there was a spare moment those few months, you know where my feet were. And there was so much to do besides being at the beach. I could've lived at the San Diego Zoo for the rest of my life and been happy. There was even a fond memory with Beau when we took the Harbor Cruise for the day. The water, the dolphins, and the salty breeze calmed us.

It seemed like we were always fighting, but that wasn't true, and our time together wasn't always horrible. I used to tell myself the reason we loved hard and fought hard was because he and I had so much passion. A broken mind will create any lie to make even the worst situation seem all right. I viewed myself pragmatically when I could. Beau was stubborn, and so was I. And I never considered myself perfect and blameless. I cussed and nagged a lot. I'm sure there were things I did that made things worse, but Beau reminded me regularly of all my shortcomings just to make sure I'd never forget.

I wish I'd learned early on that it's okay to have character flaws if you acknowledge them and attempt to change your behavior for the better. Yet Beau condemned me for each perceived flaw he could find. And he bullied and abused me for them as an excuse for his rage.

Gandhi said it best: *An eye for an eye leaves the whole world blind.* The worst part about Beau was he never allowed me to grow. He pounced on my character flaws even after I had tried to improve them in some way. Whenever he was upset with me or himself, he would resort to the same verbal assaults. I could lose twenty pounds in a month, and he'd still call me fat. Or if I got a new certification at work, I was still a dumb bitch to him. When we worked the same hours, I would do all the cooking and laundry. Yet he would call me lazy. I don't know if he ever saw the parts of me that I'd improved upon. He only commented on the bad parts, even if he had to create new ones that didn't exist.

I remember my mother telling me as a teenager, "You can be the juiciest, ripest, peach on the tree, and there are still going to be people out there who do not like peaches."

Maybe Beau didn't like peaches. Maybe I would never be what he wanted. I wish I could have accepted who I was, even if I wasn't what he wanted. I didn't know there was a view of the world beyond Beau. It was God's grace when I found someone who loved peaches later in my life. At the end of the day, you'll never be enough for the wrong person. No matter what you do to make it work out, it won't be enough. Finding yourself wanting to leave a situation doesn't mean there's something wrong with you. I think back to all the wasted years, desperately trying to change myself into a strawberry. I'm grateful for the day I realized I'd always be a peach—and a damn good one at that.

You are likely saying to yourself by now, "Why would anyone put up with all that crap? Why didn't you just run back home, Sadie?" There were two reasons: When someone owns your mind, and you feel trapped, they don't need to put you in chains. You make your own. Second, you don't know you can free yourself. Every day I was standing over a volcano, looking down, knowing I had two choices. You tread carefully, or you fall in and die.

I wasn't surprised to find out Beau knew a lot of people in San Diego. Apparently, he'd spent a lot of time there before he met me. I suspected he contacted an ex-girlfriend in the city, as he was overprotective with his phone while we stayed there. Beau always kept his phone with him, and it was always locked. He did not share passcodes with me, but he expected me to share mine with him. Years later, I found out he had gone into my phone and linked my locations with his phone. He always knew my whereabouts when we weren't around each other.

That's something I never understood. He had no reason not to trust me, because I was his pet, in a way, loyal to the extreme. His insecurities and guilty conscience became evident one of the weekends in San Diego.

He picked fights with me over nothing. Each time we argued, he would storm out. It just wasn't like him to start a fight and not finish it. So I became suspicious he was faking the fights as an escape to see someone else.

Julie was a chemical engineer from Malibu. Beau mistakenly called me her name one day while he was drinking on his way into the shower. I doubt he even realized what he said. Angry and nervous, I asked Siri on his iPhone to call Julie. This was probably why voice recognition got implemented by the phone companies. His phone said, "Okay, calling Julie Johnson." I quickly ended the call. Now I knew her full name and location, so I could easily track her down on social media.

Julie Johnson was beautiful. She had long, flowing honey-colored hair, a nice complexion, and a thin frame. She graduated from the University of Southern California, where she had joined a sorority. She was smart, beautiful, and everything I wasn't. Or so the bile flooding my stomach told me. A healthy reaction would've been to pack up and disappear before he got back. But the chains kept me in place, as I was far from healthy.

The questions raged through me: *What in the world would a girl like her want with Beau?* Then my brain threw back in my face all the reasons I had initially liked him. His cool, confident attitude had appealed to me when we first met. And his financial status gave him real clout to the unwitting. That was before I realized he was putting everything on the company credit card and was in debt to his wife and kids. But he wouldn't dare show that side of himself to this new girl. I knew he'd fool her the same way he fooled me. She would never know he was married or that he had a girlfriend too. And if he had his way, Julie would be number three.

My blood boiled over, along with any pride I had left. I decided to send her a message.

"Woman to woman, do you know someone named Beau?" That's all I texted to her so I could confirm I hadn't contacted the wrong Julie Johnson.

"Yes, what about him?" she replied.

I told her who I was, and that Beau was also married to a woman named Caroline. And I told her everything, which was far more than she needed to know. She explained how Beau had met up with her at a bar. And they had planned to hang out the coming weekend. But by the time I was done with all the unpleasant details, she was disgusted.

"You people are freaks! You are involved with a married man, and you want me to feel sorry for you? I don't feel sorry for you, because you and him deserve each other."

That was her final text before she blocked me.

I tried to convince myself I didn't care what Miss Julie "Zeta Beta Pi" Johnson had to say about me. But I admit her words did sting a little. It reinforced the idea I deserved everything I had coming to me. Worry and dread sneaked into my drunken brain. Maybe she would disappear, and this wouldn't come back and blow up in my face. But as usual, I wasn't that lucky. It didn't go away, and it blew up in my face.

Julie addressed Beau of his wrongdoings and what she thought of him before she blocked his phone number along with mine.

When Beau slammed the hotel door shut, his wrath was boiling over. You would think a man who just got caught trying to cheat would let that one go, but he didn't. This also needed to be my fault.

"I'm getting real sick of your shit, Sadie!" he shouted loud enough for the nearest rooms to hear. "I'm getting real sick of you meddling in my life, you jealous cunt. Why do you have to be such a dumb bitch all the time?"

"You met her at a bar!" She had already confirmed they had kissed the night before.

"She was a work prospect! Her company was going to put us on their bid list. Spencer is going to be awfully pissed when he learns you fucked this one up for us!"

"Are you going to mention to Spencer you tried to fuck her too? Beau, that's what this is all about, isn't it? She doesn't work for a company that bids on our real estate projects. You were never going to be added to a bid list. I am sick and tired of your lies and bullshit!"

It felt good to bark back at him, forgetting I wasn't allowed to call him out on his lies and misdeeds. This was a one-way street. Beau hated it when I reminded him he wasn't perfect. And he hated being called a liar even more. But the real kicker was when I showed him the proof.

I held up my phone like we were a rock-star celebrity couple fighting it out on TV. I took delight showing him the conversation I had captured on my phone with Julie. I assumed the truth of it all being shoved in his face would force him to apologize for the whole scene. I know—you don't have to say it. And you can probably guess what happened next.

Beau grabbed my brand-new iPhone and threw it as hard as he could on the tile floor of the bathroom. It shattered like he shattered me after our first fight. That was the seventh iPhone he had destroyed that belonged to me, but who was counting? He would just buy a new one on the company card.

"You want to make me look stupid? You want to save conversations? You want to try and hurt me? Don't forget who made you, dumb bitch! I can break you just as fast."

I thought about my options. There were few. There was no way to calm him down at that point. I couldn't run, because he would chase me down. More arguing would've been futile. If I agreed with him, he'd assume I was mocking him. Screaming would've led to him suffocating me with a pillow. So I decided to ask *him* what my options were.

"How can I fix this, Beau?" I asked. "What can I do to make you forgive me?"

"I just want you out of my life! I can't do this with you anymore. I'm tired, Sadie. And I am sick of your craziness. I'm tired of having to worry about you getting me thrown in jail. You are going to ruin my life." He inched closer with his wild smirk. "But I'd rather hang than go to prison."

"You want me to leave? Fine, I'll leave." I attempted to walk past him toward the door, but he moved fast and blocked my path. In the process, he elbowed me in the face hard enough to give me whiplash.

I screamed through the pain and tears. "You promised me you would never hit me again! You swore to me!"

I could see the craftiness behind his eyes, debating what he'd do or say next. "Come on, Sadie. You know I didn't *mean* to hit you this time. That *really* was an accident."

The knock on the door startled both of us. Someone in the hallway had overheard all the shouting and reported it. The hotel manager called the police. Beau slowly opened the door after he threatened me to keep my mouth closed. The cop asked him what was going on.

"We were just watching a loud movie, Officer. Really!"

The policeman insisted on hearing from me too. "I was in the bath."

He gave Beau a suspicious look. "I thought you said she was watching the movie with you?"

Beau stared at his feet. "No, I said I was watching a movie. She was in the bath."

"Ma'am, I'm going to need to speak with you."

I walked to the door, trying to hold my composure. As soon as the cop saw the bruise on my face, Beau was in handcuffs. "I'm going to need backup. We have a domestic situation here."

"Ma'am, are you okay? Did he hit you?" the cop asked me, still holding Beau.

"It was an accident," I said, trying hard not to cry.

"I didn't ask you if it was an accident," he said. "I asked you if he hit you. Your answer will be simple, and I will give you a hint. The answer will either be yes or no."

"Yes," I said and burst into tears.

Before I could say anything else, more cops showed up. Beau was taken away in a police car to the local jail.

Like many states, California law required me to press charges. A year after our first fight in Oklahoma, that state adopted the same law. This was the first and only time Beau went to jail for hitting me. The rest were hidden from the public and the authorities.

Beau spent two nights in jail before they allowed Sawyer to bail him out. He received an automatic restraining order. He was warned if he were to come within a hundred yards of me, he would be taken back to jail. I don't think I got any sleep those two nights he was away. When he got out of jail, he didn't come to the hotel. Sawyer called me and said the job in San Diego was wrapping up and suggested I go to Thackerville. There wasn't any compassion or questions if I was all right. The entire drive to my house, I knew

Beau would contact me to fire me. Then he'd tell me to never try to contact him again. That's what played in my broken mind over and over.

I tried calling him several times on the way, but he wouldn't answer. I spent days in my house, depressed and drinking alone. I didn't know about the restraining order. It wasn't until we were finally face-to-face in the hotel parking lot that he explained everything to me.

There was going to be a court hearing, and I would have to testify. I could choose to press charges or not. For the first time since we met, I had leverage over Beau. Yet I was still too naive and ignorant to understand the power I had.

"What about my job?" I asked.

"What about it, Sadie?" he said, annoyed.

"Is my job safe?"

"Stop asking me if you still have a job. That shit is getting old. I'm not going to fire you. Is that all you care about?"

"I don't believe you," I said.

"Look at it this way: you drop all charges against me, and I'll make sure your job stays secure."

"How can you assure me my job is safe?"

"I'll have you report to Spencer from now on. I can step down as your boss, and I won't have the authority to fire you. Spencer doesn't know about any of this. And he won't if you stay quiet."

"From now on, you're going to have to convince Spencer to keep your job." Beau walked back to his truck, then turned. "I can't protect you if you screw up anymore."

"Deal," I said without hesitation. I was good at my job and immediately liked the thought of answering to Spencer. It wouldn't be difficult to demonstrate my capabilities and stay in good standing with him and the company. That's when I wondered if Beau had been holding me back from promotions on purpose. But it wasn't long before I found out the good-ole-boy system had zero interest in how bright I shined for Spencer. Beau still ultimately decided my fate behind the scenes.

One week later, the San Diego County Sheriff's Office called me regarding the domestic assault case. I told them that I had gotten drunk and overreacted. I explained to them Beau was a good man, and I would not press any charges despite their attempt to convince me to reconsider my decision. Everything was dismissed.

In less than an hour, I received an official work email informing me to report to Spencer going forward. I took a deep breath and thought I might make it out of this situation alive. Then I remembered Beau's threats over the years about knowing all the deep holes he could drop me in.

I could have been anything in the world that I wanted to be, but I chose to be a ghost.
I allowed you to turn me into this.
Something was better than nothing with you.
I stayed loyal long after you were gone. I couldn't imagine someone else standing where I stood.

CHAPTER TWELVE
Invisible Chains

How do you know when you've hit rock bottom? When you are too ashamed to go home to see your family and friends. You make cute remarks like, *I'm just so busy!* Or you summon up a bit of energy and declare, *I'll be back after the next job!* If they detect sadness in your voice or face, you blame it on lack of sleep. Smiling beneath sunglasses was my default pic.

I was ashamed. I was still involved with a married man. And most of the time he wasn't even a good human being. I couldn't pretend he was separated anymore. Lying to yourself only lasts in front of others. Inside, there's a spotlight on all the things that cause you pain. I needed to deaden the nerves. My choice was to drink until I no longer carried resentment for myself or the company I begged to keep working for.

If you're looking for rational, think again. The invisible chains I created for myself kept me from taking any wise steps toward freedom. The den of wolves is not a pleasant place to be, but I told myself it was safer to be one of the wolves than to be a sheep. So the best thing I could do was move into the shadows and plot. To avoid focusing on myself, I needed someone else to blame, a target. I started obsessively stalking Beau's wife, Caroline.

It's amazing how much a warped mind can find out on social media, whether it is true or false findings. I wanted to see what their relationship looked like to the rest of the world. And I wondered if Beau was happily married when he wasn't with me. Had he told me the truth about anything?

Caroline posted only the highlight reels, similar to what I had been doing. No one had to ask where he was all the time. My paranoia convinced me she knew I was stalking her online. I told myself she had made sure to keep enough things public so I would see them. Every thought was about me. I glared at the pictures she posted of their children and the sappy posts on their anniversary. I knew he had spent his anniversary with me out of town, but had he sent her gifts and flowers? When I scrolled through all her photos, I wondered if she had to pretend online too. She had to be, *right?*

Beau always described Caroline to me in such a negative way I was shocked the first time I saw a photograph of her. Caroline had the simple natural beauty that every girl who had to wear makeup hated out of pure jealousy. She even looked like a celebrity. I would watch movies when I was alone and believe it was actually her on the screen. No wonder Beau married her.

That's what burned me. He had made her out to be this uneducated, ugly inside and out, money-hungry leach. She was none of those things. I often wished she was, so it would make it easier to hate her. Instead, she appeared on all accounts to be smart, funny, and a caring mother with strong Christian values. She had unblemished porcelain skin and warm chestnut hair, like a beautiful dusk over desert sand. Caroline was the exact opposite of me in every way, or at least what I thought of myself at the time.

My brain had to weigh the evidence of what I discovered about her against the picture of her Beau had painted. I wanted to believe everything he told me about her, but I didn't. He was a consummate liar of the first order. So I continued to stalk her social media, hoping I would one day figure out their complex relationship.

I couldn't comprehend why she wouldn't leave him if she knew about me. If Caroline did really know about me, why wouldn't she leave? This made me wonder why I hadn't left, and that sent me out to the store for more liquor. I wouldn't dare ponder such thoughts without my reliable coat of armor. Alcohol protected me from my self-deprecation like a tireless defender.

I plotted scenarios in my mind. If he was fooling us both, we could team up and slam the truth in his face. But I knew that wouldn't change anything. I was trapped, and she obviously still needed him too. He governed our success and the length of our chains. Was she secretly trapped too? Oh, how I wanted to speak to her about all the things that weren't mine to speak of. She was his wife. She had every right to post the high points. How dare I get jealous over the possible loss of something that never even belonged to me?

Beau and I always fought about Caroline. She called his phone ten times a day, but Beau refused to answer in front of me. On the few occasions I did get into his phone, I saw they talked a lot when I wasn't around. Caroline happened to be best friends with Alex, Sawyer's wife. That made things even more complicated. Sawyer traveled with us to every hot-spot vacation we took on the company's dime. I imagined conversations between Alex and Caroline, comparing notes and confirming their suspicions. Did they talk about me? Or were they both home just collecting large paychecks from men they never had to put up with?

As my twisted investigation dragged on, I decided Caroline was too good for Beau. But I never admitted that to anyone. So I did what any threatened, twentysomething, defeated girl would do in that situation—I highlighted all her flaws. I ranted about Caroline to Beau every chance I got. I figured if I pointed out her flaws, even if they came from his lies, it would make me shine brighter. That's the dark place where I dwelled.

I let Beau know I was jealous. She had what I wanted. I wanted to be a wife and mother one day too. I suspected she also would have traded places with me any day. And I knew she had to be jealous of me too. I flew all over the world with him while she was at home with her kids.

On days when I was only slightly inebriated, I considered the idea she stayed with Beau because she was a Christian. Obviously, I wasn't a follower of Christ back then, but I did wonder if heaven would reward her for never giving up on their marriage. Worse still, I wondered if I'd be condemned for always trying to take her place.

It was easier for me to pretend what I was doing was beyond my control. My fate was in Beau's hands. If he decided he wanted me gone, I would be gone. I was manipulated every single day that I knew him, and I felt like I couldn't walk away. Even when he told me he wanted me to leave, he would stop me when I tried. There was no escape. It reached the point where I couldn't even describe what willpower was anymore.

I shouldn't have felt the need to hurt Caroline. If I had been smarter, I could've used her help. She could have been an ally for me and me for her. I see that now, but surviving in the pack meant I had to protect my territory. Perhaps I had a little more wolf in me than I realized. If only I could've used my predatorial instincts back then; I would've been in a lot better shape. A false notion that wolves in the wild challenge their leader to keep the pack strong has been debunked. Only if the leader of the pack dies or wanders off due to old age or disease will the pack choose a new leader. When wolves come of age, they leave the pack, off to start their own family. Wolves are smart, leaving when the time is right. Instead, I foolishly imagined myself overthrowing the alpha leader.

I left work.
I seemed to have misplaced my inspiration that day.
I sat in silence as the ceiling fan hummed.
The door is locked,
and while others are searching for a way in,
I'm desperate for a way out.

CHAPTER THIRTEEN
Shame and Blame

LATE SPRING IN CASPER, WYOMING, was startling. Watching the sun set over the Rockies filled me with so much joy. It was like nature was painting the scene in front of me, and it was just for me. The fresh air was crisp and clean. When I pulled up to the hotel, I didn't want to unpack. I just stood there, trying not to blink, leaning against my Escalade.

Sunrise was just as majestic when I pulled into the heavily wooded jobsite. To everyone's surprise, Beau rolled up last in a brand-new truck hauling a brand-new RV with all the bells and whistles. I had to admit it was beautiful inside and out. It was nicer than any apartment I had ever lived in. He was the center of attention, just the way he liked it.

When I found out he had financed the whole thing with Caroline, I wanted to vomit. That obviously wasn't something a man would do while going through a divorce. Decisions like that would only keep them attached to each other.

Naturally, I checked Caroline's social media for new pics.

There it was. My heart sank to my toes. I wanted to cry. It was a picture of them with their kids. They had spent a whole week in it, driving around, staying at various well-to-do places, camping like a normal family. Images of them singing by the fire, roasting marshmallows, and laughing tortured my imagination. The pic with his arm around hers, smiling together, pushed me to the boiling point.

I confronted him with the photo as soon as we were alone. "What the hell is going on?"

Beau droned on about how he had to let her use it because she helped with the financing. There wouldn't need to be a next time, because of everyone's schedule. As always, Beau had an excuse for everything. We argued all day until he said he wanted to make it up to me by taking me to dinner.

Johnnie Walker had become my trusted armor. Wine wasn't strong enough for me by then. Most of the time there was a little ice and a whole lot of whiskey in my glass. One morning, an older lady in the office was discussing her late father and alcohol recovery. Her comment replayed in my head: *Halt! It's never a good idea to drink under duress, whether you're hungry, angry, lonely, or tired.* I should've taken that as a warning. Instead, I drank twice as much when I was tired, and three times as much when I was angry. The result always left me hungry, then I would feel lonely.

Beau seemed oblivious to my emotions. Every sip roiled my anger. After dinner, we were back at the RV. He invited me to stay with him for the duration of the project so I could pocket all the per diem money. Beau claimed he was being generous, but I suspected he was trying to take some of the pressure off him.

The layout of the RV was beautiful. The smell of the fresh

carpet alone should've made me happy. But imagining him and Caroline sharing the first memories of camping together in the RV, then posting it all on social media, triggered my rage. I lost it. I wanted to burn it down, so I whipped open several doors and cabinets to see if Caroline left anything behind, unaware of how weak the hinges were until one cabinet door broke.

Even when you drink as much as I did, there is still a pocket of awareness inside you. But instead of stopping you from doing something stupid, it mocks you after it's done. *You're going to regret that one.* I didn't need my inner voice to tell me what I already knew. I had messed up in a big way. And there was no going back.

Within seconds, Beau had knocked me to my feet. I was disoriented to begin with, then all of a sudden I was on the floor in the fetal position yet again. But this time he was in my ear, and he screamed as loud as he could.

"You dumb bitch! You have been pushing me all night! Is this what you wanted?"

I didn't answer. And I realized in a moment of clarity that I was still the child back by the bridge next to the river in Shreveport, craving attention and compassion. But the current situation with me and Beau had become so broken and destructive I had settled for negative attention. As bad as it was, it seemed better than nothing.

"You wanna break shit? I'll show you how to break shit!"

There were long seconds of darkness. It might have been minutes. I couldn't be certain of anything that was happening to my mind or body. Beau yelled in my ear over and over. I tried to stand up at one point, numb physically and emotionally. I was discombobulated, which I assumed was from the alcohol. My head was pounding, and the dizziness was like being inside a tornado. Then darkness came again.

The next morning I woke up to severe ringing in my opposite ear and dried blood inside the ear he had screamed in. My entire body was sore. I had bruises on my neck, and I struggled to swallow. I couldn't hear out of my left ear for two weeks.

I started by cleaning the blood out as best I could. I was still half in the bag when I came up with a brilliant idea. Maw-maw used to pour hydrogen peroxide into my ear. At that moment, it sounded like a good idea. It was used medicinally when I had an earache as a child, so it made some sense to try it. The instant the peroxide touched the skin in my ear canal, I jerked my head, trying to get it back out. It burned like nothing I had ever felt before. I might as well have poured scalding hot water into my head. That's when blood began to flow out of my ear.

This was one of the worst pains I'd felt, even to this day. And I've given birth.

When Beau came back inside the bedroom and saw me lying there with the blood oozing out of my skull, he rushed me to the urgent care down the road. Did it take this for him to finally care about my safety and health? Had the violent event finally ignited a feeling of remorse inside him so that he would genuinely care about me? Not a chance. He made me recite what I needed to tell the medical staff. We *agreed* on the story that I might've punctured my eardrum when I was cleaning it with a bobby pin. I then had to explain how the peroxide added to the pain, and my ear went numb. The tale seemed plausible to us. But not to the doctor. He insisted on knowing how the ear canal had gotten so inflamed.

The weak story stuck, and we left as soon as the prescription was in my hand. The doctor had put me on medicated drops for over a week to prevent infection, considering the inner wall of my ear had ruptured. The inner wall protects the eardrum itself. Each time I had to use the drops, I cried hysterically. The burning—I will never forget the burning.

"I did this to myself," I said to the pitiful image in the mirror. "I deserved it." The blame wasn't solely mine, but when you wallow in your own self-degradation, it really doesn't matter.

Anytime Beau physically hurt me, he tried to make it better by taking me on a vacation. I was too lost to understand the logic. His motivation was to hide my injuries from the public until they healed. Every physical confrontation led to two things without fail: First, I would need time to recover. Second, he'd find us somewhere to go I had never been before.

The alcoholic state of mind is an addiction like any other drug. Every alcoholic becomes a mental gymnast when it's time to assign blame. The first tactic is the easiest. Blame everything on the alcohol rather than holding yourself accountable. *A drunk man's words are a sober man's thoughts.* I don't know who came up with such a wise adage, but it's true.

Beau was Beau, sober or drunk. And he needed to shift the blame for anything in his life that might make him look bad to others. He never held himself accountable for his brutality. Not even once. *I must have been blackout drunk. I don't remember doing that.* His notorious lame and shameful excuses were never excusable. Forgive and forget is a common phrase people say to placate a person who suffered. But I doubt I will ever forgive Beau, and I will certainly never forget what he put me through.

Even on my worst day, I didn't deserve the abuse I suffered at his hands. I can see clearer now through honest eyes. But while I was with him, my thoughts were muddled. And I couldn't rely on self-esteem, as mine went into hiding long ago. It was easy for Beau to convince me that I deserved his frontier justice. And I was the one having to apologize for provoking him to hurt me just enough to teach me a lesson.

He actually sat me down at the end of each tumultuous event and made me consider all the ways I could've prevented my ass-whooping. Every condescending sermon Beau gave me was downright evil. And they all ended with a warning to keep my whore mouth shut.

My obligatory response was always a sincere-sounding apology, with a promise I'd never do it again. Just like his promise to never hit me again. It was all a bad joke, and it was always on me. After the eardrum incident, I begged him on my knees not to leave me or fire me. Memories sometimes feel more shameful than the actual moment.

"I'm so sorry I broke the cabinet door," I whispered. "I'll never do anything like that ever again."

My life choices were simple. If I hadn't broken the door, he wouldn't have been forced to hurt me. He would often tell me my biggest problem was that I couldn't control my alcohol and that I was a sloppy drunk. And he tried to soften the criticism by telling me it was because I was born into a white-trash family, and that's the reason I did not know any better.

His wolf teeth showed in his words when he wanted them to. "Caroline doesn't cuss." Or he would say, "Caroline doesn't drink. Caroline doesn't start fights. Why do you think I married someone like her? That's why I will never marry someone like you. That's why no man will ever marry you. They may fuck you, but you are not marriage material."

Those words hurt, though I never gave him the satisfaction when he said it. I wanted the white picket fence and to be a mother one day, but he even implanted the idea that no other man would want to have children with me either. I would never be a good mother. I'd be destined to raise a white-trash child, just like me. I was too damaged. I was irrational. My breath stunk. I was a fat alcoholic. I was lousy in bed. According to Beau, I had a couple of tattoos that looked like someone in prison did them.

The mirror was my final friend. I used to get drunk and look in the mirror and cry while talking to myself. "He's right, you know," the face in the mirror would say.

Immediately after the eardrum incident, we were in the Cayman Islands. I winced from the bruises while lying in a hammock. Then I dutifully posted the approved pics of my trip. And I loved reading all the comments from the people who read them.

"I want your life," one of them said.

"Are you always on vacation?" another asked with a laughing emoji.

"You are so lucky!" That was the most common post.

Obviously, it wasn't real. They were only highlight reels for my circle of friends, family, and coworkers to see. But the comments acted like a salve on my ever-wounded soul. I glanced over at Beau, and I told him the sun looked good on him. I hoped maybe he would say one thing nice to me. I was that desperate for a compliment, even from the devil himself.

I searched for validation and love more than anything. It was the same when I wanted to be loved by my first boyfriend. I wanted love from a missing father I had never met and a mother who was rarely there. People who grow up with love are more fortunate than they know. I have witnessed how often such a simple and obvious thing goes unnoticed by those who take love for granted. Like having food every day, we are concerned with minor details. But to someone who is starving, a scrap is like a banquet. Love is the most vital component to a person's life. Nothing could be more important than being loved, recognizing it, and being thankful for it.

Before I found sleep every night, I longed for a healthy love from a man who understood how to show respect for a woman. Yet I needed to understand that my abuse was never my fault. I spent the first decade of my adult life believing I was hard to love. I know now I was worthy of love, whether it was hard to love me or not. I wish someone would have told me that. Shouldn't that be taught in our homes, schools, and churches? And how can people love others if they don't know how to love themselves? I never miss an opportunity to tell young girls the true power of love and thankfulness. I've made it my mission to empower them with wisdom.

In my broken mental condition, I searched everywhere for the love I craved, except within myself. And I hoped and begged for the tiniest morsel when I was with Beau. His reaction to my compliment was silence. He never even flinched. I continued to swing in the hammock, watching the ocean waves rise and fall. That's when my thoughts grew darkest. Every "vacation" gave me a chance to envision ending it all. I imagined jumping off a deep-sea fishing boat into the ocean, knowing the swells would wrap around me as I sank. They would comfort me so I wouldn't feel ashamed, alone, and unwanted. Thinking of waves hugging me on the way down made me smile.

Beau and I oscillated between good and bad days. How drunk we both were determined if one of our bad days would result in physical abuse. But as I've said, damage to my body became easier to endure than emotional abuse. The blood dries up and bruises heal, but Beau's vile way of tormenting my mind and soul left scars I doubt will ever fully heal.

We've traveled to beaches and traveled to snow.
We've scoured the country and searched it high and low.
I don't remember colors, the sunsets, or rain.
I remember fighting and feeling insane.
Because others don't know you, they can't understand
how I can get triggered by beautiful sand.

CHAPTER FOURTEEN
The Last Acorn

I CAN'T RECALL MANY FOND MEMORIES of the times Beau took me on vacation. The dazzling scenery of morning sunlight poking through palm trees wasn't as magnificent as it should've been. Island-hopping, as Beau called it, was a direct response to physical damage done to me that couldn't be easily concealed at work. There was never heartfelt concern or remorse for how I looked or felt. Beau's public image was paramount and all that mattered.

My routine while recovering was to stare at puffy clouds, trying to make pictures out of them in my mind. I took simple pleasure in making the clouds into puppies and kittens. But the combination of physical pain and psychological erosion had taken its toll. Years of self-loathing under the onslaught of constantly being told I was nothing more than trash became as common to me as waking up.

Instead of enjoying the beautiful places we went, I categorized them by my injuries. After my busted eardrum, we went to the Cayman Islands. I bought new sunglasses for my black eyes while hiding out in Jamaica. My reward for a broken nose was a week in Aruba. Although it was warm when we were at South Padre Island, I had to wear long pants to cover the bruises that ran from my thighs to my ankles.

Yet of all things Beau destroyed in my life, self-worth was my biggest loss. Although we all use the phrase *broken heart,* I think it is overused. Romantic relationships come and go when you're young, and the breakups feel so devastating to the inexperienced. Later on, when you're a mother or a wife, love becomes difficult. When your heart is shattered with trauma and abuse, it scars for all to see for the rest of your life.

My world became bland, like watching a movie with the volume off. Worse, if I couldn't love myself, how could I truly love anyone or anything? I sat on the beaches with my feet in the sand, unable to conjure the feeling of joy I had the first time seeing the Pacific Ocean. I wiggled my toes back and forth until they were fully covered.

In general, the human species tends to congregate. Church, work, family, friends, sports, and vacations are all aspects of the clan mentality. It's in our genetic code to belong to something bigger. Yet when alone and left to our own thoughts, we talk to ourselves. That's normal. But if you're alone, and the only one you can talk to is someone you loathe, that's when dark thoughts surface to chat with you.

With the sand up to my ankles, I wondered if I should keep going. *Would anyone care if I buried myself in the sand, never to be seen or heard from again?* My inner shrug let me know I wouldn't mind. The depressing side effects of alcohol are doubly potent when combined with the PTSD from the insults and beatings. Loneliness doesn't really cut it when trying to describe the bottomless pit in your soul.

"Take my picture," Beau said as he held up a middle finger with one hand and a beer in the other.

How classy. That's what I would have said when I was a sassy bartender the day we met. But not anymore. I was like a zombie, indifferent to it all.

"I'm sending this to the guys," he said. He threw his empty bottle in the sand and picked out a new one from the cooler. "I wonder what the poor people are doing today."

His comment irked me on many levels. It's something people who aren't rich say to each other tongue-in-cheek when having a good time together somewhere special. But they're actually pointing out a form of thankfulness for their happy experience. Beau projected the firm belief he was rich and that he was better than poor people.

Internally, I ranted how easy it is to appear rich when you're spending corporate money on the sly. I wouldn't dare say what I thought of him out loud. If I had been given the choice to be rich with Beau for one day or poor by myself for eternity, I would have chosen being alone. It made me laugh to myself for a moment. It was rare I ever chose me. And though it might sound small, it turned out to be a gigantic step in my attempt to regrow my self-esteem.

I lived for Beau. I made sure he shined at work. I cleaned up his messes. It was difficult to live every day torn between who I was and who he demanded me to be. I considered it brave to accept who I was at that time in my life. Though there wasn't anything wonderful I could say about myself, I was better than Beau. I knew that much. He controlled me on a daily basis. And I abetted the crime by allowing it. Out of self-preservation, I played the painful game at my own expense. But that day, with the sand over my ankles, I started to see through his lies. That spark would lead to me being proud of myself later in life. I clung to it like a squirrel with its last, most precious acorn and tucked it away.

The final contract of the year was in Western New York. South of the Buffalo region, the Adirondack Mountains crept up from Pennsylvania. There were vast expanses of cheap land with small communities dotted about the countryside, so there had been lots of bids on the land there.

The trees in Upstate New York were like fireworks. Cooling winds blew the multicolored leaves across the sky until they blanketed the ground. The people were simple and good-natured, for the most part. They referred to the area as the Southern Tier. It was charming how they would fit right in with the laid-back customs of the rural South. I promised myself that if I ever got clear of Beau and found a way to believe in myself again, I would come back to appreciate it properly.

Fall was always my favorite time of year, even before working for Beau. I couldn't wait for the first cool front when I was young because that meant Maw-maw would let us decorate the house with pumpkins. Now it meant work was winding down for the year, and I could retreat to my house in Oklahoma. I often thought about visiting home to see my family and friends, but I'd become too smothered in shame.

When I talked to everyone on the phone, I kept it light and let them do the talking without letting on all that had happened to me. I'd ask a lot of questions to detour any focus on me. Only Abby had a sense of the trouble I was in, but she had her own life. And

I didn't want to involve her in my mess, still believing everything happening to me was my fault. I didn't want to risk her becoming entangled in the dangerous drama. And she was the only person who would come with me when it was a big weekend for Beau and a Cowboys game.

I had to keep my torture a secret. And it wasn't because of losing Beau. I feared if anyone else knew, my income would come to an end. The big paychecks kept me going during the worst of the storms with Beau. It was like holding on to the bathtub during a tornado.

I knew my mindset was as unhealthy as my drinking. I was walking a razor's edge, and if I couldn't find a job close to what I was making, then I'd lose my house. Despite all the trauma, I promised myself it was worth it. I was no longer in love with the idea of Beau. I feared him. And I feared what my life would look like without him. I worried about the girl he would one day hire to replace me. Would she be younger, prettier, skinnier, and less mouthy? Would he fly her off to the places he took me? Would he tell her all his secrets? Would she be everything I wasn't? I'll bet he wouldn't have to hit her to make her listen.

I cried hard when I thought like that. I couldn't stand the thought of the "next me" to end up in the same torture chamber I was in. Wouldn't some of her blood be on my hands for not stopping him? I was too weak to take action like a confident, self-respecting individual. It was that last acorn I kept hidden—that one tiny spark that set me on a path to undo Beau.

I started taking and saving notes on Beau and everything he did. I wrote down dates and expenses I thought were suspicious. I took photographs of all the paperwork I thought relevant. I never had a concrete plan to use them, but it was a step in the right direction. Some days I think I did it solely to keep me from going insane to the point of no return. And if Beau fired me on a given day, or blamed me for his activity, I would need proof. I might have been a defeated soul, but there was no way in hell I would ever take the fall for him.

It's scary to feel alone
in a place that feels haunted.
Because I haven't lived in one place yet
where I ever felt wanted.
I feel like it will take forever
before I ever get ahead.
And by the time it kills me
I'd just as soon be dead.

CHAPTER FIFTEEN
Under the Thumb

My suspicions were confirmed as I watched Beau closely. Many of his day-to-day tasks at work seemed illegal. I might not be the one to get him fired, but I could make sure I was not signing off on any of those dealings. I did not have the time nor willpower to incriminate him. All I wanted was to have records and proof I was not a criminal. *All is fair in love and war,* the saying goes. I imagined whoever was responsible for that quote had dated someone like Beau in their past.

My goal wasn't even to hurt Beau. I wasn't looking for revenge. All I wanted was freedom. I wanted to keep my job, should I choose to leave him, while having the option to move on with my life without consequence. Whatever label one could put on our relationship, *toxic* was always the first thing that came to my mind. Having sex with a boss was obviously playing with fire, but the volatile nature of the situation had me scheming for a way out of his clutches. I wanted to escape without losing everything. I wanted to maintain my status with the company or work in a similar role with a similar company.

I only had four years of experience in the field. I worked in a portable building for every jobsite in the middle of nowhere all over the country. I was mentally and physically exhausted. The idea of traveling the country became less appealing as time went on. Under Beau's thumb, I was wearing down. But there was something else gnawing at me in the background. The carefree aspirations of a twenty-year-old bartender had been subtlety and naturally replaced by a shaken woman of twenty-five who had begun to realize time wasn't her friend. I can't say the biological clock was ticking inside me then and there, but it was definitely winding up.

The notion of settling down was looking better and better. When I was alone and drinking at night, I started fantasizing about marriage and children. Through my blurry, bloodshot eyes, I became a heroine in a movie, trying to escape the deadly obstacles. I longed to leave in the dead of night, sneaking away to find the male hero. He'd be a real man who would love me the way I had always yearned to be loved. We would get married, have babies, and buy a proverbial brick house with a white picket fence. Our little family would eat dinner at the table together. Then my magnificent, handsome husband and I would crawl in bed together, sober. He'd watch the news while I read a book. And he'd always be there to come to my rescue when the villain tracked me down in an attempt to spoil my happily ever after.

Hangovers the next morning were rude awakenings, returning me to the painful reality of my life with Beau. In my spare time, I'd secretly look at other job opportunities, searching for a possibility to escape the situation I had trapped myself in. Daydreaming about my freedom never lasted long enough, as my thoughts would get interrupted by anxiety. Without fail, my innermost thoughts took me to the dark place of my memories, where I stored Beau's confessions of *ending me* during his many drunken rages. I had no doubt he would make good on his threats.

"I'll drive you to the Mexico border! And I'll bury you so deep they won't find you until you're a fossil! And I have plenty of people who will help me do it, and others will be my alibi."

He wasn't lying. Through the years, he'd paid a lot of rough people a lot of money. If he asked, they'd do whatever he wanted. So our routine went on for a while longer. The chains that held me were invisible, but they were stronger than my beaten will.

Although his imagery for my demise was dark, my depression and addiction made it even darker. When curled in a fetal position, I just wanted it to end and waited for him to kill me. And fighting with Beau was impossible because it wasn't enough to hurt me by exploiting my many insecurities. Not only did he want to make me cry but he also wanted to make sure I knew how crazy he would become. If I crossed him or went too far, I'd be a goner.

Beau started fights by saying things that forced me to disagree with him. Then he would take a threatening position and turn up the volume of the argument. There were no tactics I could use to diffuse the bomb. Siding with him was ridiculing him. I couldn't agree or disagree. And if I tried to be silent, it made him angrier. He needed me to react to his evil. I just had to take what he gave me and prayed it passed quickly.

It was never quick though. By the time it was over, I would want to rip my own hair out, assuming he hadn't already done that for me. In my mind, Beau transformed from someone who I thought was beautifully broken to believing he was hideously evil. He took pleasure in inflicting pain on me in every conceivable way until I was certain he was the devil himself.

Out of nowhere, good fortune came my way when the company offered me a permanent position in the corporate office. I wasn't sure if it was God's divine intervention, recognition of my hard work by Spencer, or just dumb luck. It didn't matter, because I was thrilled to have some stability in my life.

As much as I loved my first home, I listed it for sale that autumn. If it sold, I could buy another home in Tennessee, where the company had an office specifically created for all the big southeastern projects. The idea of working alongside a lot of other women in the office gave me a sense of security. Beau couldn't fool them forever if they saw him every day. That was part of the reason I think he was so loved and well respected. No one got to see him every day. He could be wherever and whoever he wanted to be at all times.

All they saw were the number of jobs we were being awarded. They didn't see how much of the company's money he was spending, and it wasn't my job to show them. But I listened and kept secret the information I had been gathering. I wanted the ladies to witness firsthand the real me and the real him.

Beau had a way of putting on a show for the women in the office. He often walked in the building midmorning with undetected whiskey in his coffee cup, still hungover from the previous night. Everyone assumed he had been busy, returning from a successful field visit. And his crew would never rat him out. If any of them were unaware enough to make a snide comment or joke about Beau's whereabouts, they would be fired the next day.

The new office was enormous, at least by the standards I'd seen working for the company over the years. Even Beau was impressed by the available space and couldn't wait to put his evil touch on it. Shortly after we moved in, it looked more like an upscale version of a frat house than a corporate office. Beau had added a foosball table, a beer fridge, and a rock-climbing wall in the warehouse.

A week later he added an outside kitchen for daily cooking and entertainment. The area was fully equipped with outdoor TVs and surround sound to watch football. There was a stocked liquor cabinet in the outside kitchen and the community break room. Beau also had a decanter in his office filled with a rare and expensive single-malt whiskey.

It was common to see someone making a Bloody Mary or mimosa before the sun was up. After work, the guys usually stuck around and played foosball or poker like a pregame warm-up before they went out to the bars all night long. Two thousand dollars, at minimum, was spent on alcohol every week using my company card, along with Beau's and Sawyer's.

Imagine my surprise when I got my first real job several years later. I had to relearn how to be a functional adult. The realization that the rest of the business world didn't operate the way Beau ran things was total culture shock. Looking back, I don't know how everyone else thought it was normal to have a stocked bar in the break room. I'm guessing they didn't, but no one was bold enough to bring it up in staff meetings.

No one challenged Beau's spending or his day-to-day activities. And I was too naive and controlled to do or say otherwise. I knew I was on a short leash with him. I already had a strange upbringing with alcohol, so drinking all the time seemed justified, as if it were the norm. Though everyone drank, no one did at the level of me and Beau. They had to have wondered how either of us could even function. Unlike me, they knew what the appropriate time was to start drinking and when it was time to stop. Knowing when to stop wasn't in my learned behavior catalog. You stopped drinking when you either passed out or ran out. That was my norm.

Upon taking the new office position, I was expected to perform important tasks reflecting the changes at the corporate office. The restructuring of the company at the top level had created a new team to look at the financials. These individuals ran a tight ship, comparatively speaking, considering the last bunch didn't ask many questions or expect much from the guys in the field, especially field supervision. Beau's reaction was no surprise to me when the new controller and accountant team demanded his receipts so they could allocate his spending appropriately. Were the winds finally changing in my favor? I could only hope.

I could always tell when he was lying.
He would talk on the side of his mouth, exposing his canines.
I couldn't help but torture myself with the burning question:
Did you crawl out of her holding on to everything you could
never find in me?

CHAPTER SIXTEEN

The Devil's Due

Beau didn't particularly care for anyone in the accounting department at the corporate office. He didn't like anyone who challenged him. He wasted no time bumping heads with the people who asked questions from a billing perspective. Beau practiced his arguments for Spencer to have all of them fired. He didn't know I was listening. His arrogance and bullying knew no bounds.

It was well known throughout the company that if Beau didn't like you, then it wouldn't take long for you to be fired. No one escaped his wrath. After his verbal and email confrontations with the corporate finance office, the vice president came out to site to fire Beau. By the time he left, he'd given Beau a promotion. That's how smooth of a talker Beau was when cornered. He can argue and manipulate anyone. Even though Beau got a raise, the vice president had challenged him. So Beau immediately started plotting against him.

Within weeks of the attempt to fire Beau, the vice president was let go. He used a lot of his loyal contacts to plant evidence and talk poorly about the unwitting man. The whole thing was over before it had started. From that point on, no one dared cross or question Beau. This led to an increase in the already out-of-control spending and misconduct. He knew no one could stop him now. And Beau let everyone know it. He bragged about it like he was marking his territory.

Yet this overconfidence made me wonder if it would be his undoing in the end. The tasks given to me in my new assignment revolved around allocating Beau's spending before it went to the accounting department. That's right. He got to decide how he would turn in his expenses, with me as the go-between.

If a purchase hit the reports at midnight, Beau had me assign it to the "appropriate" code at 12:01 a.m. He supplied me with a list of codes to make the spending look legitimate. He would say things like, "Hey, I just booked a flight. Code that purchase to job showing."

Once I completed my end of the subterfuge, I'd see the email confirmation of his booked flight to Cancun. Although we never worked real estate gigs in Mexico, I did what I was told and coded it as a job showing. From that moment on, I wondered if he was setting me up just in case he got caught. Talk about a rock and a hard place. If I did what Beau told me, I was complicit in the fraud. If I didn't do what he said, he would fire me and possibly say I was embezzling funds.

The biggest danger for Beau should have been the IRS. They weren't people he could bully into submission. I didn't understand how tax reporting worked for our company. And it made me wonder if I would be charged for misallocating funds with fraudulent purchases. Those questions kept me up at night. And drinking was the only way to make it go away until the next day.

After six months in my new position, I had gained a new perspective on all aspects of the company. I saw firsthand the importance of the field and why they needed so much job tracking and documentation. I also got a behind-the-scenes glance into Beau's spending. While I cleaned up Beau's messes, he tasked me with allocating Sawyer's spending as well.

It took almost two days from the time they swiped their company card before it showed up in a report that was sent out to upper management. From there, accounting had to determine how to code those costs for the monthly financial breakdowns. I assigned the costs as soon as it posted so no one would question them. Beau told the corporate heads he assigned me to take care of it because I was working in the field and in the office. And even though I reported to Spencer, I was still Beau's assistant. I traveled with him most of the time; therefore I had the receipts, as far as anyone knew. That was the trap! I never saw a single receipt from any of the crew.

In the rare event I wasn't with Beau at a jobsite, I still knew where he was, when he spent money, and how he spent the money. I basically always had tabs on him, which made it difficult for him to hide anything from me, and I liked that.

Our time at the office was short-lived. A project was kicking off in northern Georgia, and they wanted me to work on-site. Beau offered to oversee the operations, and they liked that idea. Large bids had been placed on the lands around the jobsite, so there was big money at stake for the company.

I stayed with Beau in the honeymoon suites while everyone pocketed the money created by finishing the job early and with less than what had been budgeted. And Beau set the inflated budget. It was the perfect scam. I can't lie: I enjoyed living the good life. I tried to forget it was at the company's expense. My soul needed some fun.

Most of the crew who Beau liked had RVs and parked in the back lot of the hotel. On the nights that we didn't go to a fancy restaurant, we grilled out then played board games. Or we sat around and gambled for a cash pot. The guys would get drunk outside almost every night. I have no idea how they made it to work and spent all day in the blistering heat.

One fateful night, someone brought moonshine and passed it around. And I'm not talking about the fruity stuff you can find in the tourist towns in Tennessee. That night we all drank what is accurately called *white lightning*.

We passed around the jar while we listened to country music. That night, while I stared at the star-filled sky, everyone started talking about politics. Maybe I had grown up to be more like my grandfather and his union buddies after all. Out of nowhere, Beau went on a wild rant about the benefits of killing off other races and doing away with gay rights.

I looked at him with pure disgust. My stomach churned when he got like that. Beau hated women, gays, Blacks, and anyone else who wasn't a white man who thought like him. He would tell everyone what he'd do if he were president. He boasted about which countries he'd nuke and the groups he wanted to enslave. During those ugliest of moments, I speculated Beau and Hitler would probably get along when they met up in hell.

"The worst thing our country ever did was elect Abe Lincoln," Beau said as he spit in the fire. "He abolished slavery. I'll bet if he saw all the niggers running around in this country today, he would roll over in his grave." He nodded as if proud of that statement. Then he made sure all the guys nodded in agreement, regardless of how uncomfortable they may have felt.

"Beau, it's late," I said with a disapproving tone. "I think you've had enough."

"Fuck you, woman!" His eyes had that wild look, and I knew what it meant. "Don't you dare interrupt men when they speak!"

I didn't say anything else. I got up and went inside the hotel. I couldn't listen to any more of his toxic, racist, hatred. Beau stayed outside several more hours drinking with the crew before he stumbled inside the room, drunk and meaner than a hornet you just swatted and missed.

Only two things ever happened whenever Beau was that drunk. I went to sleep, hoping it was one of those times he was so incoherent that he passed out on the floor. Instead, he woke me up from a dead sleep to tell me he didn't appreciate me disagreeing with him outside in front of the guys. And it was time for him to remind me of my lot in life.

"You tried to make me look weak," he muttered with a slurring snarl. "I don't let a bitch who is one of my grunts argue with me. And a woman should never get away with back talkin' a grown man. That shit is written in the Bible, so you obey me!"

"I'm getting out," I said, shaking my head. "I don't want to be here anymore."

As I turned to leave, he grabbed me by my ponytail and threw me to the ground. I ended up wrestling with him on the floor, fighting to break free. That was the first time in all our fights that he didn't slap me. He used his balled-up fist and was intentional.

Within a second of the blow to my face, everything around us was splattered with blood from my nose. Both of my eyes were blackened in less than a minute. I staggered to the door, but Beau grabbed my shirt from behind and dragged me into the bathroom. Then he forced me into the shower, fully dressed. He sprayed my face with cold water. I'm not sure if it was anticipation or the old memories of previous beatings that caused me to keep my PTSD medication handy.

"I know you want me to go back to jail, but I'm not gonna let that happen."

He was too far gone to realize washing away my blood wouldn't wash away the evidence he'd assaulted me. And I shook from the freezing cold water. Between the water pouring into my nose and blood filling up my mouth, I thought I was going to drown.

Thirty minutes later, he turned the water off. By the time he was done, my throat was raw and burning from crying so hard. My abs ached from shivering, and a piercing pain shot from my nose to my temples.

"Now get your ass undressed and into bed." He stood there, making sure I would comply with his order.

Fear and exhaustion forced my zombie mind to do as he said. Beau passed out hard once he laid down. I listened to him snoring for an hour while I still shook under the covers. As usual, I contemplated running. But where would I go? No one would believe me. He had washed away all the blood. They would just arrest me because I was drunk and hysterical. In the end, he would blame it all on me. Beau would contradict me, and the good old boys would testify that I was the one lying. There was no way to win and no way out.

I went to sleep that night in excruciating pain. When I woke up the next morning, I could barely open my eyes. My face was swollen, and I resembled Sloth from *The Goonies.* My nose was broken, and I had two hideous black eyes.

Not one soul knew what was happening behind closed doors or even his potential embezzlement of the company's assets. Each day I sat there with my mouth shut, simply obeying his orders, yet somehow bad karma found its way to me again, and the devil had his due.

"I guess I need to pack for the beach," I whispered to myself as a single tear ran down my cheek. I was surprised there were any left.

I left behind a bread-crumb trail of hope and strength
to lead me back out of the living hell I was lost in.
Tomorrow the world will awaken with a fresh start.
That should have given me hope, yet it caused me anxiety.
In the grand scheme of things, I was a mere speck of dust in a navy-blue sky,
created from dust and one day to return.
If there were strengths I was not yet using,
I did not know I had inherited them.

CHAPTER SEVENTEEN
The Vicious Cycle of Insecurity

SOME DAYS I DID NOT HAVE THE STRENGTH or willpower to survive. Did I need Beau's permission to survive? If I left in the middle of the night, would I have a fair head start in an attempt to outrun him? Where would I run? I wish I could've cradled the little girl inside me so I could wrap love and truth around her. *It will be okay. I promise.* Sadly, I lacked the wisdom and energy to reach inward. I had no idea who Beau was anymore. He traveled through back alleyways between boy and man, human and wolf.

Winter was a blur of bruises, pain, humiliation, and drinking it away. And spring arrived faster than normal. I prayed the new year would bring me the warmth that left my heart. Winter was cold in so many ways. I would like to say nothing eventful happened that year. My life was so toxic and chaotic, but I had become accustomed to the abuse cycle, as if it were normal. I'm sure everyone looking in from the outside thought I was crazy.

I despise how recklessly the word *crazy* is tossed about. What does *crazy* even mean? If you look it up in a dictionary, you'll notice it's slanted toward females. Acting crazy and being clinically crazy are two different things. Unhealthy is what I was. Trapped. Frightened. Beaten. Did that make me crazy? Is broken the same as insanity?

Abuse comes in many forms. And sometimes it comes in repeated tiny stabs. Beau had a way of making me jealous, and it was deliberate. In my splintered mind, I would become jealous when he compared me to other women. Is jealousy a form of craziness? His evil insults were part of his control, especially when he was upset with me.

When I first met Beau, I was in the best shape of my life. I got so many compliments on my figure. I was never one of those stick-figure, runway-model types. I was curvy in all the right ways, inherited from my maternal grandmother. Though I received a lot of attention for the size of my chest, it became an insecurity. People can be so cruel, men and women. Ridiculing young people can have a devastating effect. Intentional or not, social media has turned the world into an impossible competition for what is beautiful and attractive.

Women born with flat chests are often insecure about it. But I was on the opposite end of that seesaw. The attention I got from men caused women to say bad things about me. And I wasn't one to flaunt what I had. And I never liked the howls from the boys in school or the men on the jobsites. Every date I went on was a battle to keep the guy's gaze higher than my neck. At a young age, an attractive girl starts questioning her worth.

During my bartending days, I typically wore tennis skirts with polo shirts to work. It was a comfortable outfit, flattering on me, yet it didn't make me appear to be *asking for it.* I worked hard to keep my figure. I played golf and tennis several times a week back then. I'd go for long walks in the woods and watched what I ate for the most part. When I took my first project out of town with Beau, I packed my golf clubs. He wasted no time to start breaking me down.

"Golf is a man's sport," he'd say with disgust. "You aren't even that good. You just like the attention because that skirt shows your ass. People probably think you're just a dyke bitch."

None of these things were true, but at this early point in our relationship, Beau's playful manner still had venom. His hurtful comments were effective because I would return to my hotel room in a sour mood, wondering if people did think I was an attention seeker. At first I thought Beau had no reason to lie or to intentionally hurt me. He likely picked me out, knowing I was too naive and ignorant to see the red flags. So there I was, in front of the hotel mirror, pantomiming golf swings to see if my skirt was really that short.

His heartless attack had found its mark. I stopped golfing. His poison had infiltrated my bloodstream. After that, Beau forbode me to wear yoga pants or any athletic shorts and skirts. So I wore only jeans. Yet no matter how good I thought I looked, he still refused to compliment me. Before I realized it, I'd given up everything and everyone Beau didn't approve of. Giving in was easier than fighting.

After four years, I knew what triggered him. And I knew when he was getting jealous or violent. It was the only predictable thing about Beau. This is why my life looked so chaotic, and I may have appeared to be the jealous and possessive type. Beau was my whole world because he forced me to make my world smaller. I wasn't jealous. I was being manipulated.

He would parade women in my face who I should've been friends with. He'd invite wives of inspectors and coworkers and compliment them right in front of me. When we were alone and both drunk for different reasons, he'd tell me he either had sex or wanted to have sex with them. The next day he'd laugh at me, confessing he made it up just to mess with me.

By that time it was too late. I had already gotten mad at him in front of strangers. And it didn't matter I'd always been a girl's girl, because he constantly made me fight other women for his attention. Then he would tell me it was my own fault I didn't have any real friends. If you've never been in an abusive situation—and I pray you never have that experience—it's more than impossible to describe how the smallest things can open a massive wound, over and over.

I wanted to scream sometimes, thinking of all the girlfriends I had until I met him. I just stopped arguing with him. I stopped talking to my family. I stopped calling and texting friends. I put an end to all the activities I once enjoyed. I let Beau place me in solitary confinement.

Thankfully, for my *sanity*, Sawyer had a new girlfriend every week. I was able to double-date with them—per Beau's approval, of course. But even that was tricky. If Sawyer told everyone a joke, and I laughed too hard, Beau would later accuse me of wanting to sleep with him.

"If I'm such a whore, who is fat and can't get along with anyone, why do you want me?" I'd scream at him while wiping away my tears. My question was a small way of fighting back. I should've known he was evil for making me cry without remorse. Instead, he would stare at me with a look of triumph in his eyes.

"Because I see your potential," he often said in those moments. His games were heartless and cruel. It was easier for me to smile and agree with anything he said while ignoring all other forms of human existence. I began gaining weight as a result of inactivity, depression, and a poor diet. I felt like I got in trouble for everything I wore when I was in the best shape of my life. But when I had put on unwanted weight, he never missed an opportunity to remind me of that too.

Though Beau's two favorite nicknames for me were "dumb bitch" and "fat whore," "trashy cunt" was a close third. He'd curse at me after coming back from his private affairs, then accuse me of screwing someone else while he'd been gone. It took exhaustive promises that I had been home the entire time before he'd let it go. It was ridiculous. And when would I have the time to screw someone else? I already had a jam-packed schedule between all the self-loathing, anxiety, PTSD, depression, body dysmorphia, and my full-time job. I could barely fit in my insomnia, so there wasn't any time at all to see anyone else, much less another man.

Occasionally, I channeled what little strength I had into the one thing that didn't piss him off. Decorating my home was something Beau appreciated. I spent over thirty grand one year on furniture and decorations. I'd spend countless hours on Pinterest and online shops like Etsy and Home Goods.

"Caroline lets dogs sleep in the house," he said from time to time. "And she is the worst slob I've ever met. At least you keep a clean home."

A compliment? No, it was just another sly comparison to Caroline. It was one of many of his artful jabs at my psyche, reminding me he was married. The worst part is, I allowed it. And I let my brain continue to dwell on the differences between me and his wife. Anything I lacked she possessed and vice versa. Jealousy grew as ideas of myself diminished and ideas of who she was crept in. She had to be as mentally exhausted as I was, which often made me wonder if Beau was physically abusive with her. I could never figure out why he complained so much, considering he had the best of both worlds, with two slave women to flip back and forth to whenever he wanted.

Then one day I was reading Beau's emails, and I saw one from Spencer.

"Sorry, I'm running late," Spencer wrote. "I'm having a rough morning."

"It's okay, pal," Beau wrote back. "Look on the bright side. You could be walking in my shoes with a wife and a girlfriend who are both in competition to see who can get fatter faster."

I don't know what hurt more: Beau's words or Spencer's laughing reply. I would like to think this was more of a witness to his character than mine and Caroline's. We weren't lazy, we weren't slobs, we weren't fat. We were simply miserable and unfulfilled.

I believe that's why I focused on something I took pleasure in, something without fear of retribution. Interior design and donuts kept me from going completely numb inside. I knew if it weren't for that, I would have no reason to live at all. When you're in the abyss, you grab hold of whatever small victories you can.

Even though my idea of happiness was distorted,
I still managed to see with eyes that viewed the world through a lens of gratefulness.
I never knew who my real friends were. Life had become so messy and without warning.
I hated admitting that when I looked in the mirror I could see my mother's eyes staring back at me.
I didn't know this was something I should find endearing.
After all, she had faced a brutal world and managed to survive when others could not.
Trust was tricky. I did not trust anyone, including myself.
There were moments when I would reflect on my circumstances and had no one else to blame but me.
I put myself here and now. I just needed to learn to love this version of me.
What was left of me.

CHAPTER EIGHTEEN
Evil Within

"Where does this go, Sadie?" Reese asked, holding up the box game of *Pictionary.*

"Over there on the bookshelf near the window," I said. "And thanks again for helping out today."

We were unpacking boxes in my new home in a suburb of Knoxville just in time for early spring. My first house in Thackerville was sold on Valentine's Day, so I set down new roots in a small cottage home near corporate headquarters in Tennessee. A couple of the ladies in the main office came over one Sunday to help me move in.

I was so thankful to be making friends in the office. And it was refreshing to have normal conversations with like-minded women. It took them a few weeks to warm up to me. They knew about Beau, and that I was his girlfriend. I didn't hold it against them for watching what they did and said around me. I laughed it away as much as I could, assuring them they never had to act a certain way in front of me. After that conversation, they relaxed and took me into the fold.

Soon we were all laughing and joking each day in the office. The work camaraderie had a healing effect on me. I always tried to be genuine with them. I'll always be the type of girl who wears her emotions on the outside. In those days, I couldn't hide how I was feeling, good or bad, no matter how much I wanted. It felt reassuring to have a semisafe haven.

Beau and I both had our own office in Tennessee. The first contract for the year kept both of us away most of the time while we were out on assignment. "On assignment" to him meant we could take advantage of company funds to travel wherever he wanted. During that period, Beau flaunted his unchallenged power by taking us on glamorous vacations, and we spent little time at the jobsites. Every expense was paid for by the company, whether they knew it or not. And not a single person questioned us.

At that point the only person Beau answered to was Spencer. The only person I answered to was Beau. Spencer knew we traveled for work and pleasure, using our company cards. It was the company's way of thanking him for all the new work he brought in, according to Beau. Even though I didn't believe him, I had witnessed firsthand how many contract bids ended up with our company. The business he generated was substantial.

Beau always knew just the right people wherever we went. He was able to manipulate his contacts to bid on the jobs. That was how he always had the inside track for the surveying and all the other things the crew did. As Beau's ego grew, so did his lust for spending. We usually took two big vacations per year. The shorter ones were to hide the damage done to me. But his newest display of power had us flying to five-star hotels and exotic resorts. We only had to spend a few days at a new site to establish his presence, then we were off to someplace fun. The combination of our salaries and having all expenses paid by the company still wasn't enough to sate him.

He started using the company card at stores that could easily say had been for purchasing supplies for the jobsites. But he was actually spending it on gold and silver. Drastically inflating the cost of the supplies allowed him to pocket a handsome sum every week to purchase precious metals. Beau was building his own private nest egg. Because I was allocating the costs to routine job numbers and safety supplies, no one dared confront him. I knew what we did was wrong and could one day lead to big trouble. But I was on that invisible chain, and it was better than being dead and buried in a hole somewhere.

If I ever mentioned to Beau that it seemed like we were stealing, he insisted Spencer had given him the green light as part of a bonus agreement. If that were the case, why did I have to lie on the area that I allocated the receipt? I wanted to ask him that, but my instincts told me to play along while keeping a diary of things I thought could come back to incriminate me.

I liked knowing where he swiped his card. It made me feel like I had a little power of my own to know where he was when we were apart. The jealousy in my mind wanted to make sure he wasn't cheating on me with a different girlfriend. How sickening that sounds to me now as I look back. I realize how perverted my life was during that time. I worried he was cheating on me whenever we were not in the same place. Meanwhile, I was the girlfriend of a cheating married man, who was still my boss, regardless of how the company had it on paper. In the wilderness I was in, I did whatever I could to survive and keep my rank in the wolf pack. Questioning the leader of the pack was death. Leaving the pack was death.

Beau stayed with me in Tennessee, and he'd go home once every three months to see his kids. We only fought about Caroline every time he went home. Beyond that, I ignored the topic. I knew that conversation would only lead to fighting and pain. And I convinced myself daily that I was fortunate he was living with me, and I shouldn't push my luck.

I wish I could go back and shake that girl—the girl I had become. I wish I could shake her and wake her up. It was certainly confusing to knowingly take part in corporate fraud while I had a relationship with Beau. The two aspects were intertwined. To separate one would break both. In the end, I would be the one broken into smithereens if I rebelled.

During that period, I didn't question Beau about his spending or what he did during the time he spent with Caroline. Every now and then, especially on birthdays and holidays, he kept me on his leash by placating me with $500 in untraceable cash. I had a hunch the company had unwittingly paid for my gifts, but I never turned them down either. If I didn't spend it on myself or things for the house, it would have made him suspicious. It was his simple way to incriminate me, but all I could do was follow along.

"Your hands are dirty too," Beau said during one of our drunken arguments. I'm not sure we had any arguments when we weren't partially drunk. Partially drunk is partially sober. That's just more of an addict's mental gymnastics.

When I threatened to call human resources, Beau reminded me how he could make me vanish.

"My boys south of the border will make you disappear without a trace, and no dog would have a nose strong enough to pick up your scent."

Beau had taken on a few young Hispanic workers early on that season and mixed them in with the regular crew. No one noticed but me. Then he let it slip one day they had ties to the drug cartels. Just more of his drunken boasting, or so I thought. Soon after he made that comment, Beau received an envelope from some of the unruly workers. *Happy Belated Birthday* written on an envelope was put on his desk. They had gathered thousands of dollars in cash and gave it to him as a gift. The truth became obvious when it became a monthly "birthday" present.

It was clear Beau had formed a solid relationship with some unsavory people who came from dark places. I wholeheartedly believe to this day Beau could've had me killed at any time. My body would be gone, decomposing while he told some tale of me running away drunk. The good old boys would all have the same story, and I would eventually be a cold case.

When his threats reached that level during the bouts of physical abuse, his eyes would go black. His whole face would change. His eyes would be locked on mine, glaring without blinking as his fists hit me. The evil inside him enjoyed it, as if he were possessed in those moments. I'd watch him look down on me as I lied on the floor, battered and bloody as he spit on me. He was devoid of the slightest empathy for me before, during, or after. If he let out any sense of regret or guilt, it was faked to manipulate me.

Beau told me once if he killed me by accident, he would claim insanity and walk away. I also knew if he planned it, he would have someone else do it for him. He would have it done in a way that he could have a solid alibi.

The scariest part that made the threat real was I hadn't told anyone about the mental and physical abuse. How could I convince anyone how evil he was if I stayed in the situation for so long? No one would believe me.

"It's not about what you know, Sadie Crowe. It's about what you can prove." He reminded me of that often, and I took note of his words.

I was thankful he was out of town when I had a miscarriage. I didn't want him to blame that on me too. I did not know how to feel. I was alone one night, and my stomach was cramping worse than I'd ever felt before. It was worse than severe menstrual cramps. With every passing minute, they got worse, and that's when the bleeding started. It was much more than the normal period blood. My monthly cycle was the only predictable thing in my life, and I knew something had to be wrong when I missed a period weeks before.

I attempted to be Dr. Google and look up reasons for a missed period on the internet. And other than the obvious, I read that stress could easily influence your cycle. So I chalked it up to stress, and I didn't take a pregnancy test. Beau and I had only been intimate once in the previous two months, when we were both blackout drunk. On that night, we obviously had misplaced our resentments.

As the pain intensified, something seemed more than wrong. It hurt far worse than usual, and I was bleeding far worse than usual. I rushed myself to the nearest hospital and learned I was in the middle of a miscarriage. I was flooded with mixed emotions. Someday in the future, away from the life I was in, I still planned to want and have children. But did I want to be tied to Beau for the rest of my life? This was the first time I really thought about my future with Beau and the company. The miscarriage added to the list of things haunting my dreams at night. *Did I lose the baby because of alcohol? Was it the stress of my relationship with Beau? Had this happened due to being assaulted?* There were so many nights I didn't even consciously remember being hit.

I never told Beau or anyone else about the miscarriage. I could bear the pressure of blame and ridicule. I knew I was unhealthy in every aspect of my life. And I knew I wasn't capable of being a mother—just like Beau reminded me all too often. I was just a dumb drunk who could never raise children and have a successful marriage. Hell, my body wouldn't even allow it. The one thing a woman is supposed to be able to do—bear children, be fruitful, and multiply—I couldn't accomplish. Even my womb knew I was trash. I buried the pain where I wouldn't have to face it.

I sit outside for the first time in years.
I've lost my sense of color.
Not a cloud in the sky, and it smells like autumn.
I can't see the leaves change to burnt umber.
I wonder why no one gets sad when the leaves die.
Watching them fall makes them appear brave.
They say enjoy life while you're living.
Tell that to the leaves unsung
I crunch beneath my feet.

CHAPTER NINETEEN
Dark Abyss

SUMMER FADED AWAY, and October seemed chillier than the previous years. And I wondered if my blood had become colder after surviving another a year of the abuse cycle. I had lost count of the fights and the fake vacations that followed. I drank away the pain, wallowing in the memories of the hard life I had lived. Little did I know what lie ahead.

We projected to triple the amount of work from years past. Beau was still living with me, and we had traveled all over the country for "work." When we finished the final jobsite, Spencer and corporate were happy with the results.

As if deciding on what to eat for breakfast, Beau casually claimed it was time for him to take the proper legal steps to finalize the divorce process with Caroline. His kids were nearly out of high school, so he could leave without impacting their lives too much. I didn't believe him at all. I'd heard it so many times; I could only offer an obligatory nod.

Imagine my shock when it actually happened. And I think the

kids were just as shocked as Caroline. At first glance, you'd think this was a pleasant turn of events for me. Instead, I was more frightened than ever. Change of that magnitude could mean the end of my situation. Beau and I had gone through the motions the whole year. We were in the same room, but we were as far away from each other as an owl is to the moon.

The fighting had decreased in frequency out of boredom, at least from my perspective. I couldn't remember if it had been more than a year since we were intimate. There was no music or laughter when we were drunk and on the road. Whatever the situation had been between Beau and I was now stagnant. We took care of required business during the day, barely spoke, then we drank ourselves to sleep every night. Even Beau's passion for fighting had fizzled out by the end of summer.

I didn't care enough about him to get mad over the small stuff anymore. For some reason, I thought we could go on this way forever. I couldn't understand why I wanted it to go on. I had to react to Beau for so long in order to survive, and that's all I knew. Maybe it was as simple as that. I pondered the concept of slave mentality. Historically, freed slaves often returned to their captor. Many of them never left at all. I think I understood how they felt. It was all they knew. Change can be frightening, even if it is positive. There are many facets to insecurity and fear of abandonment. And I had a lifetime supply of both.

I questioned if it was possible to accept this way of life and continue to work side by side with Beau. Ennui had set in, and I was drinking more than ever before. That's quite a statement, considering my history with alcohol. I didn't even bother with wine anymore or making whiskey mixers. One ice cube melted in the rest of the glass of whiskey became my go-to. I didn't care if it was good whiskey or cheap. Whatever I had in the cupboard was all I needed.

I was packing on the pounds, and I was barely eating anything. I contemplated switching to wine, but I would need a lot to reach my buzz. And I needed the buzz to get me through each day. I worried the ladies at work had noticed my extra perfume and nervous tick of eating breath mints. I shifted to expensive scotch, the smooth kind that barely leaves a scent of alcohol. I told myself how clever I was to the face in the mirror. My vision was too blurry to see it clearly.

Beau had to take a lot of trips to Tyler, Texas, to sign divorce papers and meet up with the lawyers for both sides. He also had to visit his aging grandfather, who had fallen ill. I persisted in my obsession of checking to see where Beau was swiping his company card. In my drunken fits at night, when I was alone, I'd accuse him in my mind of cheating on me. I had become a paranoid drunk, depressed, and desperate.

"You found someone else!" I'd yell at the empty room. "You're going to replace me with a younger, skinnier, newer me!" I honestly didn't care at all if he fell in love with someone else. I wasn't in love with him. I still wanted someone who would love me the way they do in movies. I wanted a fairy-tale romance—a great love story. But I was a caged pet in Beau's ruthless world.

After crying myself to sleep each night, I'd wake up to the reality of having to pay double the mortgage in Tennessee than I had in Oklahoma. And I had financed a sports car on a drunken whim earlier that year. One destructively dumb decision after another. The company had offered me a car in the summer to drive, so I kept the sports car for fun. I had put almost all my cash into the new house and all the needless furnishings. There was no way to save money.

I know now all that behavior was a distraction so I wouldn't have to time to focus on my depression. I had become hyperfocused on decorating once the house was fully furnished. I felt anxious that I wouldn't have anything else to do by myself, so I started binge-shopping for every holiday decoration you can imagine. My entire garage became a holiday warehouse. And I'll bet I was the only person in the country who had a table setting for Flag Day.

I never wanted to take a day off from work, and I dreaded company paid holidays. I'd be left alone in an empty house. Sometimes I poured two glasses, pretending someone was drinking with me. I was still a prisoner. If I left, Beau would know about it. He had a tracker on my phone and Lord knows where else. It wasn't worth the fight. It's not that he still wanted me; I was a possession. And I still needed more experience and a recommendation when it was time to leave.

Beau sort of owned the company by proxy and ruled the industry. He knew everyone, and I didn't have one connection who wasn't connected to him. I wanted to network out on my own, away from his influence, but it seemed impossible at the time. At minimum, everyone knew me as Beau's assistant and some joked they would steal me away from him because they knew how hard I worked. I knew if I ever reached out to any of these men, they would likely hire me until they spoke to Beau. It didn't matter how well I performed or how many certifications I received. I was his property—that much was known.

Whiskey and holiday decorating were my only defense

mechanisms against my frequent and crippling panic attacks. The only happy pause from my sorrow was when Abby visited me. She flew to see me several times when Beau wasn't there, especially when I confided how lonely I'd become.

Other than that, my life was utterly isolated. Because of Beau, I didn't have many friends or relatives I could call when I felt like my world was crashing down on me. They thought I was selfish. They saw me as a haughty world traveler who was too shallow or thoughtless to show up for weddings or showers.

Midsummer, I informed Beau I was going to Louisiana to see Maw-maw for Christmas. I argued with him to the point of exhaustion. The next thing I knew, I had a black eye, sitting on a nameless beach. From my friends' point of view, I chose to go to the beach instead of their baby showers. I seemed like a self-absorbed bragger on social media. Beau liked that I posted highlight reels. It was his protection to demonstrate he wasn't abusing me. That made him feel like a high roller, as if I were bragging to our friends. How sickening.

I was not depressed before I met Beau. I could not recognize if I was experiencing dark depression, or if I had lost my happiness. But there are so many subtleties to chronic depression. I called it the *dark abyss.* And my mind was forced to visit with it when things were at their worst. I couldn't remember what it was like to be held or loved. And I knew something was breaking, and it wasn't my heart. That had been shattered too many times, so I knew what that felt like. This was different. I had wandered into real darkness. The abyss of your subconscious has a way of talking back to you when it's really the last thing you need. That is how you know you're in serious trouble.

"Am I unworthy of love?" I'd ask while pouring another glass.

I can't think of any other reason.

"Am I even a good person anymore?"

I think you know the answer to that.

"Do I have any friends left?"

The room is empty, as always.

My life was in a free fall, though no one on the outside knew. I was living a lie, and it was impossible to walk away. I started drinking more during the day. I couldn't stand to hear my own thoughts anymore. I had an anxiety attack at work one day, so I walked into the break room. The stocked bar was always available. I took one shot to calm down.

More than seven shots were needed that day to keep me from breaking down in front of everyone. But the more I drank, the more emotional I got. Some days I'd close my door and just cry at my desk for hours. Beau only came into the office once a week; then he would leave again. It was cold, a burning cold, the way ice feels on skin when held there too long. I had wanted to be away from him for so long that I couldn't understand why it was eating away at my psyche.

My addiction reached the point where I was having to replenish the bar at the office and stock the house on a weekly basis. There were others who drank at work. But it would be over a celebration of some kind, or they just wanted to party during the day if their workload was light. They all needed a nudge to take a shot during the workday. Not me. I needed to drink. It was the only way I could survive. At least, that's what I told myself.

With little sleep and barely eating, the only fluid I took in was from the whiskey. That's when dehydration kicked in. My often unwashed hair began to fall out, and my cracking lips had dabs of blood. My skin started to wrinkle in areas I hadn't noticed before, as if I were a stranger in the mirror. When I started to vomit blood in the mornings, I realized I had developed ulcers from stress and alcohol. I had no idea where I stood with Beau or the company. Living in constant fear and anxiety had eroded every part of my life. I used to find relief thinking alcohol might one day kill me. That dark thought was no longer challenged by the voice inside my head.

As a kid, I imagined death was a sudden event. As a drunk adult, death was like a rope I was barely hanging on to, watching it slowly fray one string at a time.

It's not pretty watching a pretty girl fade away.
You watch her grow up innocent, and then you watch her make mistakes.
You wish you could hold her and take away her pain
as she is pouring another one of her dreams down the drain.
It's not pretty watching a pretty girl cry.
You watch her light up the room, and then you watch her say goodbye.
As she gets in the car, you wish you could stop her.
She's hurting herself again, and you hate to see her suffer.
It's not pretty when she's older, and she has no one else to blame.
You watch her run away and then come back home again.
It's not pretty watching her try to love,
never really knowing what she is deserving of.
She knows deep down she is alone in another strange city,
just praying to be saved from a life that's not pretty.

CHAPTER TWENTY
The Decision

WINTER TURNED MEAN, as it sometimes does. Yet I clung to the notion the next year would be better. Beau hadn't been at my home with me for weeks, though he managed to make an appearance or two at the office. He had to maintain his profile. I rang in the New Year sloppy drunk, sitting alone and miserable on my back porch watching the fireworks.

My alcohol addiction had reached the critical stage. Instead of just drinking every night, I descended into drinking all day, every day. As soon as I sensed the alcohol wearing off, I needed another shot. And I was never the type of drinker who always had to have a drink in my hand. Alcohol had become my shield so I could numb the ugly emotions I didn't want to feel. I wasn't addicted to alcohol. Technically, my addiction was masking the fear and loathing in my mind. That's all it takes. One reason to get the avalanche rolling, then it's just a matter of time until you're buried.

I took shots to suppress my anxiety and fear, then kept taking them throughout the day to remain numb. I was aware of what

I was doing the entire time, but we are creatures of habit. So, when any form of addiction sets in, your mind will do anything to convince you it's okay to keep going. I thought of it like sitting outside during a hurricane and telling myself I have no choice, and everything will be fine. When I looked over the sky and tasted the rain and wind, I realized the storm was going to sweep in and take me with it. And there were days I didn't care if it did. It was the only alternative to allowing the smallest emotion to unsettle me. Alcohol or death.

The mind is a powerful thing, and when it's broken, it can do a lot of damage. If anxiety set in, I took a shot of whiskey. Loneliness, that was another shot. Guilt awarded me two shots. I started each day with a half glass before leaving for work, then I sneaked shots in during the day. When it was time to go, I rushed home to an empty house. I would lay on the couch and drink to myself in silence. I didn't even turn on the TV or the radio. If the phone rang, and it wasn't Beau, I didn't answer. I'd only answer if it was him. Not out of love. I answered out of sheer panic, but his calling frequency decreased as my panic intensified. He knew the prison I sat in was secure.

Most mornings I woke up around 3:00 a.m. with a stiff neck from the couch. My stomach was always angry and hungry. I'd just tell myself my body knew it was time for another drink to settle my nerves. My king-size bed reminded me how lonely I was, so I avoided the bedroom as much as I could after several panic attacks. Some nights I would settle for a pillow on the floor with a sleeping bag. But the couch seemed safe, and I had a clear view of the driveway.

I watched the driveway, drinking and staring with the remote hope Beau would arrive to check on me. Like I said, he was all I knew. Every night that I was disappointed meant I earned another shot. I sat there like a kid waiting to be picked up by a parent who never showed up.

Abandonment is not easily described. And there isn't a quick fix. Like your shadow, you turn around, and it's there. You can't always remember how it got there, but you can't get rid of it. And everyone reacts differently to their abandonment. My solution was obvious.

I would drink shots to keep the tears away and would blackout eventually. My alarm was set for 7:00 a.m., and I threatened it many mornings. Regardless of how exhausted and sick I was, I found a way to get to work on time for a while. I don't know if I forced myself to go to work out of fear of losing my job or if it was the slim chance Beau might show up in the office. Maybe it was a combination. Regardless, I'd get myself together—well, half together—and drive in.

I started coming in late when I started having panic attacks in the parking lot. I would sit there, parked in the back of the lot beneath the trees. Drinking was the only way I could get past the shaking and sweating. Once I marshaled enough courage, I would walk in late, smelling like a brewery. Then I walked straight past my office into the break room, where I would pour another shot as a reward for making it that far.

This was the first time I realized I had begun to resent my job. Prior to that, I always told myself I was hanging on to my job out of fear of losing my one success. The high-paying gig had been the first thing that made me feel like a worthy, successful, and contributing part of society. It provided respect with my family, which is something I had yearned for since I was a child. As I descended into the shadows, the job became a burden.

I couldn't look at the stranger in the mirror anymore, because I didn't want to face what I was becoming. And I didn't want to listen to the voice inside my head that was telling me what I was transforming into. I knew my skin was turning leatherlike and weathered. I didn't need any reminders my beauty was eroding with every shot of whiskey.

It's true what they say: you never know what someone else is going through, so you should be kind to everyone. I thought back to my first day of work with the company and all the men I judged without knowing them. I thought about their weathered faces, then wondered how hard their lives had been. During my bartending days, I could spot a drunk before I could smell them. I wasn't aware enough to wonder what had happened to them or how they got to be in such a situation. I used to believe drinking was a decision when I was a naive, wild teenager. While I was in the addiction cycle, I wasn't making any decisions. Every moment was a reaction from a previous reaction and so on.

When I was only drinking at night, it was easier for me to conceal my alcoholism because I was a normal social drinker, as far as anyone knew, and it wasn't affecting my work. But once I started drinking all day and night, then I knew every shot might be my last.

Despite my downturn at work and the rumor mill that followed me everywhere, Beau still managed to lift my spirits when he visited the office. One day he called and told me the reason he needed to spend more time at home. He was going through a midlife crisis. We talked while sitting on the couch. He felt worn out going through the divorce, his aunt had just passed away, and his teenage son had been arrested for assault. Apples don't fall far from the tree. The sudden attention Beau gave me by confiding his troubles placated me. And in the sorry shape I was in, I believed him. Really, he was just checking on me, making sure I was still his prisoner. Oh, and I was.

Then two more months went by without him even speaking to me, let alone staying at the house, so I made a decision. The next time Beau came to Tennessee to visit the office, I told him I wanted him to move out. I wanted to move on with my life. I wanted him to realize he couldn't take me for granted. I assumed his reaction would be to get mad and come back to the house, not wanting to lose his pet. I was so lost in depression and alcoholism, I truly believed that would be his decision because he'd be afraid to lose me. But he wasn't.

He walked out of my office without arguing or trying to change my mind. He didn't even say goodbye. At first I thought he'd left my office because he was upset. While I sat at my desk, wondering what his lack of reaction meant, I saw him gathering his things on my home security cameras. He was moving out of my house. I was so startled it was all over. I never believed in a million years he would move out for good.

I called his phone fifty times before I left work and drove home as fast as I could. I had to stop him before he left. When I pulled into the driveway, he was gone. I walked inside my empty home the same way I had done for the past several months, but this time it was hauntingly silent.

I stood in my walk-in closet, where all his clothes had once hung—the same clothes that used to remind me that we weren't over, and he would be back. My soul was so tortured, bruised, and battered, I led myself to believe there was still hope for us. Not hope for love. Rather, it was a hope that there was still a path for me to walk. But hope was long gone, and so was Beau.

There was nothing left in the house that belonged to him. Beau must have taken all the good memories because I couldn't even find one. I collapsed to the floor in my closet. I laid there on the floor and cried for hours, feeling sorry for myself. I'm not sure what caused the most anxiety at that moment. Beau wasn't a friend and never deserved that title. But he was all I knew, and without him, I was completely alone. Losing him and the thought of losing my livelihood put me in a tailspin I couldn't recover from.

It was a Friday afternoon when all this took place. I knew it was going to be a long, sad, lonely, weekend. When no more tears could come out, I drove to the liquor store down the road and placed five half gallons of cheap whiskey at the register.

"Someone's having a party," the cashier said with a smile.

"Oh yeah," I said, unable to hide my sarcasm as I handed the cashier my company credit card. "It's going to be an all-nighter."

I was determined to scrub your scent off me,
only to feel regret afterward.
Without your scent lingering on my skin,
how would I know you were really ever here?
When you left me,
you forgot to unchain me.
Who was going to feed my fear now that you are gone?
Will I starve, or will I gnaw on my own flesh?

CHAPTER TWENTY-ONE

Reese

MY HEAD WAS POUNDING, and I couldn't open my eyes. As I tried to get off the floor, some of the pounding was knocking at the front door. *Go away!* I couldn't speak out loud. It was probably a salesman or someone's kid offering to mow the lawn that hadn't been touched since Beau's last visit.

I had no recollection of the day before. I was aware I was in my own house, yet I couldn't understand why I was on the floor in my pajamas. The house reeked of alcohol, and so did I. My mouth tasted like dragon's breath. It took an enormous amount of energy to get to my feet with the help of the couch. I wandered to the still-knocking door, unaware of the day or time.

I opened the door to see Reese's familiar face. She was the only real friend I had confided in at the office. I knew she would be on my side, while everyone else would side with Beau if we parted ways. Reese was closing in on fifty and was like a mother figure to me, or at least what I imagined a wholesome mother would be like. She had a genuinely good heart. Though I told her some of my situation, I think she knew I was still hiding a lot of things. She always watched over me at the office, even though I pretended like I didn't notice. She made me feel safe, and that was important.

"Hi, Reese," I mumbled, squinting from the sunlight. "What brings you out this way on a Saturday morning?"

Reese stepped in and wrapped her arms around me as if I'd been gone for years. "Thank God you're all right. But I must say, you look and smell terrible."

Only a true friend would keep hugging someone who smelled as bad as I did.

"We've all been worried about you," Reese said, finally stepping back. She shut the door and surveyed the mess of empty bottles.

"Come in," I said, looking for the couch and secretly hoping there was something left in the bottle of whiskey half-stuffed in the cushion. "Sorry about the mess."

"When was the last time you showered?"

"Yesterday, before work." I made the mistake of lifting my underarm to smell it.

"Sadie, today is not Saturday," Reese said with concern. "It's Monday afternoon. I knew something was really wrong when you didn't show up at work today. No one has seen you since you stormed out of the office Friday morning. I've been calling you all weekend, and we've been worried something bad happened to you."

"Monday?" I plopped myself down on the couch, trying to ignore the voice in my head. *Tell her to go away! We just need a drink!* "I'm not sure where I put my phone."

Reese was still standing.

I weathered the vertigo as I got back up and went to the kitchen. "Maybe I left it in here." I wanted to pour myself another shot of whiskey, but only empty bottles were scattered around. I clenched my fists and leaned against the counter.

"Sadie, what's wrong?"

"Why did you dump out my whiskey?" My accusation would've been louder if my throat wasn't so raw from dehydration.

"Baby girl, I didn't dump out anything. I just got here, remember?"

I stared at the clock and saw that Reese was right. It was indeed 4:00 p.m. on Monday. That meant I had no recollection of my life between noon on Friday to her knocking on my door. But one thing was clear: I managed to drink five half gallons of whiskey by myself.

I started shaking. I was going to end up like the homeless population who lived under the bridge back in Shreveport. I was beyond frightened and fell into Reese's arms.

"Everything will be okay," she said while I sobbed. "I'll help you."

"Please help me find my phone, and please drive me to the liquor store."

That's what came out of my mouth. It made sense to me at the time. When I look back on that moment, it still gives me shivers.

Reese refused to drive me to get more whiskey initially. But I convinced her it might be dangerous to cut me off cold turkey. She conceded when I told her about reading an article that alcoholics often die from seizures if they attempt to quit drinking on their own.

"I'll drive you to the store on one condition," Reese said. "When we get back, you will sit down and tell me everything that's going on with you. You've let me in on a few things, but not enough to cover the rumors about you at work. People are worried about you."

I nodded, not knowing how to explain how worried I was about me. But I think she knew. I found my phone on the floor in my closet, where I had fallen to my knees on Friday. It was dead, of course. When I plugged it in to the charger, I saw the missed thirty-three calls and texts.

I was obviously still drunk but felt I was loved after all. "I want to get help." I offered her a shot as I poured one for myself.

"You need to take the first step," Reese said.

"I thought that step one was admitting you had a problem," I said with a nervous laugh.

"I'm glad to see you still have your sense of humor." Reese kept the concerned look in her eyes.

The next day Reese stood next to me and held my hand while I told Spencer and all the ladies in the office that I was in a bad place. I told them I wanted to get some help at an alcohol treatment center in California, and I needed to check myself in to get sober.

The center offered a thirty-day program, plus one week for detox. If I didn't take drastic action, Beau wouldn't need to bury me in a hole. I'd be dead already. And five weeks away from work, Beau, my empty house, and my couch would be healthy for me too.

I delegated all my tasks. The ladies were supportive and wished me well. Reese drove me to the airport and promised to pick me up when I got back. I was frightened of what was going to happen to me as I sipped on a glass of wine at the airport. Yet I was even more terrified what I might do if I didn't have access to alcohol. The part of my soul still fighting to live was eager to sit down with doctors and counselors. I needed to let them peel back the layers of my brain and see if they could see the parts that Beau had destroyed.

My treatment began the next day. On the way, my phone rang. It was Beau, demanding to know why I was checking myself into rehab. He knew I had a severe drinking problem as much as he did. He wasn't asking out of concern for me. He was concerned about how it would affect him and his reputation.

"I'm ashamed of myself. And I'm ashamed of how my life has turned out. You should be too."

There was silence.

"Beau, it's time I made some serious changes."

"Do what you have to do, but I can't say what things will be like when you get back," he said and hung up.

Did he just threaten my position with the company because I was checking myself in for rehab? Spencer wasn't thrilled with me leaving either. He claimed it was a bad time to be out of the office during the busy season, as if that were more important than someone's life.

Besides the obvious fact I was an alcoholic, I also suffered from crippling anxiety, with a heavy undertow of depression. I was in the darkest of places emotionally and physically. And I needed some solitude. My secret hope was the center would teach me how to find peace with the destructive thoughts in my head while living with a sober mind.

The five weeks in the rehab center changed my life. It was the longest run of days that I'd been without alcohol since I was fifteen. I learned about myself and the chemicals in my brain. I told the therapists everything. I told them my deepest fears. They learned everything about Beau and the last eight years of my life with him.

The therapy focused on my childhood. They wanted to expose the roots of the weeds that led me to where I found myself. After all my sober confessions, I was shocked the therapists said there wasn't anything wrong with me. They did not diagnose me with a mental illness. I was, by their account, certifiably sane. No one could call me crazy, because I had the best professionals in the industry tell me that I wasn't.

The underpinning of my addiction stemmed from my PTSD. The doctors placed me on a mild antidepressant and set me up with an outpatient program in Tennessee. I could go back and maintain my sobriety when I returned home.

I thought Beau had torn out and extinguished all the pride I had in me, but there was still a bit hiding in the shadows that rehab rekindled. Admittedly, I was sad to leave the clinic. I had made some amazing friendships with other patients. We all received a reality check together as we completed the program.

I was proud of myself for the first time since I had accepted the job to work with Beau, but in a different way. This was an accomplishment I had earned all on my own, and it was beautiful. Successfully finishing the program provided me with a special confidence, and I didn't want to let go of it. Though it would be a challenge, I had to get back to my job with my newfound inner strength.

I smiled to myself on the flight back. I looked forward to meetings with a local therapist who would help me bolster healthy defense mechanisms. I was starting to feel like myself again—the real me. She was a welcome stranger. For the first time since I met Beau, my programmed brain broke away from his label of me being a dumb bitch. I was ready to take back my life.

When I landed, I called Reese and thanked her with all my heart and soul.

I wanted to view the world as beautiful.
But I couldn't understand why the caged bird sings.
I wanted to break free of my own cage
and not be bonded to him by earthly things.
I wanted to twist the silver lining.
I wanted to downplay the entire ordeal.
I wanted to forget the sting of your fist.
I never have and never will.

CHAPTER TWENTY-TWO
Wrong Again

"I SHOULD HAVE KNOWN BETTER," I said as I hung up the phone with Beau. Every time I thought he might show sympathy, compassion, or a little concern for my well-being, I was disappointed. It was like Lucy pulling the football away from Charlie Brown, over and over.

Beau had called me the day I got home from the treatment center.

"The company had to do some restructuring while you were gone," he said in a cold, hard voice. "They eliminated your position in the office. You need to start working in the field again. You're expected to be in Holly Springs, Mississippi, in four days. If you don't go, I'll consider it your resignation."

Beau hung up before I could argue or complain. *Could he do this?* The malignant anxiety wrapped its arms around me like a straitjacket.

"Do not drink. Do not drink." That was the mantra playing in my head while I sat on the couch and contemplated my options. I should have known better to think I could ever stay with the company and have a successful life. Beau would never allow me to have peace or happiness. Beau was a taker. He took everything he could from me, and it was never enough.

Beau texted me. "I won't be going to the jobsite. Pack up and leave. I'll call you in a few days."

"I don't think I can go to Mississippi, Beau," I texted back. "I'm already scheduled to be in an outpatient program here in town. I need to be here for a while. If you can't give me the time that I need, then I'll give you my two weeks' notice. Just give me a letter of recommendation and a positive reference. I'll go work for another construction company." I assumed he'd give me at least that much, especially if he wanted me out of his life. I was wrong again.

"No, you aren't gonna work for anyone in this industry again. I'll see to that. You won't get a letter or a reference. You've got two options: go to Mississippi or resign."

I called Beau. If he heard my voice, he might be more reasonable. But he had blocked my number. Why was he treating me like this? Why couldn't he just let me go?

I felt defeated. The anxiety, depression, and PTSD flooded back with vengeance. I could tell I was about to hyperventilate as I fell on my couch and cradled my head in my hands. I stared at the ceiling in disbelief that Beau had convinced the company to eliminate my office position so he could demote me. I had sought out lifesaving medical attention, and this was his response. I wish I'd known at the time his actions were in direct contrast to my rights as an employee and a human being.

Once again, Beau had control of my life. After attending my first day at the rehab center in Tennessee, I went home and packed a bag. This was against medical advice, but I prepared to leave for

Mississippi the next day. I told the counselor the panic attacks had returned. Mercifully, the doctor sent me home with one bottle of depression medication, one bottle for anxiety, and a bottle of sleeping pills to help me stay on schedule.

If you've never been addicted to a negative substance, you're more fortunate than you'll ever know. And I pray you don't have to experience what I did that night. I had to cover my ears, trying to block the voice that was begging me to just take a sip of anything alcoholic to calm me down. My subconscious researched all the ingredients of bathroom supplies I might have had in the house. *Did I have any NyQuil, 10 percent alcohol? Maybe I should go check. Did I have any mouthwash? It wouldn't be like I was drinking again. Just take the edge off to get some sleep.*

I can't say if God was watching over me. Maybe I had just enough willpower in reserve to stay sober that night while I packed my suitcase. I realized I'd never been to a job in the field without Beau. He was sending me out to a site with an all-Hispanic crew, and I was not bilingual. Is this what he intended all along? He told me he would have me buried in a hole. And Mississippi wasn't *that* far from the Mexican border.

Were they affiliated with the cartel? Was Beau finally going to have me killed? Horrible scenarios poked at my frail resolve. Then my phone rang. It was Sawyer. Why was he calling me so late? The only times he called was when he was doing Beau's bidding.

My hands shook as I answered. "Hello?"

"Sadie, how the hell are ya?" Sawyer was drunk.

"I'm okay." I didn't want to say anything until I knew why he was calling.

"I guess you heard the news. How are ya takin' it?"

"What news?" My hands shook harder.

"You haven't heard about Beau and Caroline?"

Anger and fear churned in my head and stomach. "What about them?"

"Beau finally got free of Caroline and is engaged to some chick named *Julie Johnson*."

I dropped the phone.

It's what I always feared. Once Beau found a gullible replacement, it would be the end of me. All the pieces clicked into place. I could envision Beau sweet-talking Julie after the incident in San Diego. He told her I was crazy and attacked him. And he must have stayed in contact with Julie the whole time, promising her all the things he had promised me. That's why he didn't want me attending rehab sessions. He planned to fire me for poor work performance. But I threw a wrench in his plans by going to California for treatment.

By eliminating my position and putting me into the field, he could get the crew to vouch for him that I wasn't suitable for the job anymore. I'd witnessed this same act over a dozen times with other people. Beau was unscrupulous on every level.

I connected all the dots while I drove the next day, and I was sick to my stomach when I arrived in Mississippi. As soon as I got to Holly Springs, I found a liquor store. I got two gallons of whiskey, and I started drinking. One shot after another, and each gave me strength.

Comfortably drunk and numb, I stared at my phone for the longest time. But each second was like an hour. I picked up my phone and called the human resources manager. And I told her everything. I don't know if it was courageous, foolish, or the right thing to do. Once I broke the dam, the floodwater didn't stop. It was total word vomit. I detailed Beau's extensive abuse, and I told her I suspected he was stealing a lot of money from the company. In the midst of stumbling around the room, half-crying, and half-screaming, I lost my balance, fell over the ottoman, then soiled my pants. The call disconnected with human resources.

Before I could get to the bathroom to clean myself up, Beau texted me. Human resources had already told him everything.

"You better sleep with one eye open." Beau knew I turned him in and would retaliate for my betrayal. He knew where I was staying. I did not know one soul in town.

I drank until my whole body was shaking. I thought human resources was confidential. I thought they were supposed to protect me. How could this be legal?

I was exhausted with life. My career was finished. I wouldn't feel safe wherever I went. I had spent ten grand on rehab and relapsed on day three. He was free of Caroline and had already proposed to someone else. Beau had left me for a prettier, younger, smarter version of me.

I spent all those years with a man who swore he was going to marry me when he left his wife, only to give my ring to a stranger in San Diego. I was hundreds of miles from my house, but I didn't even know what home meant anymore. Thanks to him and my own cowardice, I had turned my back on all my friends and family. My conversation with human resources guaranteed I would be terminated. There would be no way for me to pay for my mortgage or car. And Beau was certain to have me killed because I had just ratted him out in the worst of ways. I sat there in soiled pants, feeling disgusting, fat, dumb, foolish, and pathetic. *I am and always will be a drunk, uneducated, unlovable creature. I don't belong.*

I didn't want to be alive anymore, but I'd be damned if I'd allow Beau to take anything else from me. That's the thing about givers and takers. It is up to the giver to set the boundaries because takers don't have any. The voice in my head was emboldened.

He is going to kill you. Don't give him the satisfaction. Do it your way. On your terms. If he kills you, he will gloat over you while you die.

I opened the bottle of sleeping pills rehab gave me, and I swallowed all thirty pills. I took several shots of whiskey as I waited for them to kick in. I called Reese, who'd been a real friend to me and helped me get into rehab. I thanked her and hung up. I called Maw-maw and told her I loved her. Then I called my mom through my tears.

"I'm sorry, Mama." Then sleep took me.

I woke up hours later in a hospital bed. I was alive. My cousin and my mother had spoken and managed to call the hotel I was in. The hotel called 911. The staff got into my room first, and the ambulance crew helped me vomit most of the pills. But I don't remember any of that. I could only remember waking up in the hospital, alone but at peace. *The horrible nightmare is finally over,* I thought to myself. *Beau can't hurt me anymore. I'm safe.*

By the time the doctor released me from the hospital, I had nowhere to go. Beau had my company vehicle picked up from the hotel when I didn't show up to work that morning. He made sure everyone knew I relapsed and was drunk. He didn't mention I had attempted to take my own life. I couldn't be certain he was aware I tried. But I knew he wouldn't care. If anything, he'd be upset I hadn't been successful. Dead lips can't sing.

I was in Mississippi with no vehicle. Everything I had taken with me had been thrown in a pile because the hotel had kicked me out. Beau had the company collect anything I had on me and at my house that was theirs. I forgot he still had the key. My computer, company phone, and the company credit card were gone. At least they'd left me what remained of the whiskey among the pile of clothes on top of my suitcase.

I had no idea where I might end up for the night, but at least I had my whiskey.

We all have demons; they come in different addictions.
They do not discriminate, and they know no restrictions.
They really aren't so different after all.
They all want to kill you and laugh when you fall.
Demons are tricky because they don't arrive in black or look haunted.
They come dressed in everything you've always wanted.

CHAPTER TWENTY-THREE

Opening the Door

Of all people, my mother drove to the hotel and picked me up. When we made it to my house in Tennessee, she decided to stay with me for a week. The plan was to pack up my things, sell the house, and go live with her in Louisiana until I could stabilize myself.

My mother hadn't given me the attention a child needs while growing up, and I think she felt guilty and wanted to make amends. And maybe she wanted to show me she loved me. That thought soothed my fragile mind. Whatever the reason, she had come to my rescue in my darkest moment.

She obviously knew I had been struggling with alcohol, but she didn't know any details of the tortured life I'd kept hidden for almost a decade. I didn't confide in her at first. Crawling out of the avalanche of pain was the best I could do at that time. I couldn't bear to see the same pain mirrored in her eyes. Every memory filled me with shame.

I kept apologizing for my suicide attempt as if it were an

inconvenience to her. I felt guilty she was stuck at my house on suicide watch because I needed a babysitter. My reality was still so warped that I truly believed I owed her an apology for my mental breakdown. I knew in my heart I wasn't going to hurt myself, but I felt safe with her sleeping next to me.

"I wish you'd tell me what's really going on, Sadie-Cat," she whispered. "I'll be here for you when you're ready."

I loved it when she called me that. I felt little again in that moment. It took me back to my early days, when I craved peace and love in a more innocent way. And I was being taken care of for the first time, which allowed me to rest my broken body and brain.

"I have an appointment tomorrow. Will you go with me?" I asked.

"Of course I will," she said, looking concerned. "What kind of appointment is it?"

"I have a meeting with an attorney. I just want to see if I have a case. I don't really want to get into it right now, but I'll just need some extra support tomorrow."

"I'll be with you every step of the way." She didn't ask any other questions.

The rest of the night was exactly what I needed. We watched movies and caught up on all the gossip of things going on back home. We laughed looking at pictures, pointing out how many of my friends had babies who looked exactly like they did when we were little. Where did the last ten years of my life go? I prayed that no one would find out about what took place in Mississippi. And I hoped no one would find out I'd checked into an alcohol treatment center. Beau had done a flawless job brainwashing me. I was still more concerned with putting on a show for my social media accounts than my own health.

It's a surreal society we live in. The modern world grooms all of us at an early age to care more about what others think about us, even total strangers, than learning to love ourselves. We are taught to sweep things under the rug and put on a show for the public. Sweeping things under the rug had caused my life to look like a landfill, and it was beginning to overflow. My world of fear and self-loathing mixed with guilt. How many children learn outward appearances make or break you? If you don't fit in, you are cast out.

I like to imagine what Earth would be like if all children everywhere were taught how life is precious and beautiful right from the start. And that no one is above another. The only solution to change the paradigm that I can see is to look inside. Turn off the news. Love yourself and treat yourself with kindness, then share it. We need to fix our own light bulbs inside so we can shine as brightly as we can. It may sound corny, but it's a start.

The next morning I received a few texts from people I had not spoken with in years. Out of nowhere, I was being sent love and prayers to get well. Everyone knew somehow. I should've been grateful, but instead I wanted to crawl into my couch and hide. I wanted to fade away into my own darkness like I had so many times before.

"I can never show my face again," I said to the mirror. I managed to find the strength to brush my unwashed hair and apply makeup to the dark circles under my eyes. My hazel eyes had once sparkled with all the possibilities and opportunities the world had to offer. They didn't look as green anymore. I noticed spots of yellow and traces of red where I must have strained too hard while vomiting. I missed the way they used to light up like an amber autumn sunset. I still didn't recognize the woman in the mirror, but I was determined to bring her back from the brink. Then I might be able to bring the real me back to life.

I put on lipstick and poured two shots of whiskey into a thermos. I laughed to myself as if that would be enough. So I added three more shots, some ice, and enough diet soda to conceal at least some of the scent.

"Are you ready, Mama? I don't want to be late to my appointment."

"Yes, Sadie-Cat."

I suspected my mother knew I was carrying whiskey in my thermos, but she didn't mention it. I was immediately thankful for not feeling judged or guilty. Little did she know I was carrying a lot more than alcohol in my diet soda. I carried a heavy load of years filled with abuse and self-destruction. And I was about to tell my story out loud to both her and an attorney.

Whiskey, my brave shield, needed to go to war with me. I needed it to be strong enough to share my side of the story. But the voice was still there, inside festering. It knew I needed the whiskey as a safety net in case I was rejected and tossed out by the attorney. Fear of rejection is what drove me away from most opportunities, but today it was the exact opposite. The fear of me being dismissed was bubbling to the surface, but my need to be heard was greater.

While my mother drove us to the appointment, I thought back to the stories about family drama. That's what I called it when I was a kid. Now I knew it for what it really was. One of my aunts was domestically abused. I spent the night at their house once with my uncle screaming at her. I remember him calling her vile names.

I knew she was hurting, but her only concern was protecting us. This ugly play repeated itself every time I visited. Then one day she came over to Maw-maw's house crying hysterically. I remember hearing through her sobs, *This time it's really over.*

I was too young and naive to understand the magnitude of what she was dealing with. But I do now. He divorced her, which I thought was a good thing, considering how he treated her. As a young teenager, I was confused as to why she was so distraught by his decision. My aunt was a sweet person, in my mind. She should've been relieved to be free of his abuse. I found out I had a lot more in common with my mother's sister than I had realized.

My aunt got married a few months after graduating from high school. She had zero work experience and didn't have a college education. She didn't have a phone or a car. She didn't even have a driver's license. My uncle had kept her isolated, trapped. I knew all about that. She didn't know she could survive without him. They got divorced when he told her he was leaving her for someone else. But she couldn't afford the house or the bills. She was being abandoned while he was taking away her children. It was all so familiar to me when I heard the story. Thankful Beau and I had no children together, I could still sympathize with my aunt. I know how scary that must have been for her. In that moment, I understood why I was not meant to be pregnant.

Looking back at my ignorant youth, I can't believe I ever judged a single person who had stayed in a situation that was harmful to them. Our tortured minds usually betray us in the storm of unrelenting trauma. We convince ourselves to hang on to the things and people that have hurt us. The destructive voices take advantage within the bone-chilling silence of being alone. Then the torment reverberates long after each incident like ripples on the surface of a still pond.

For the abused, insecurities, character defects, and fears cripple us, bolstering the notion we aren't worthy of a better life. I never thought I would ever meet another man who would love me. Beau had me convinced I had been lucky to have what I did with him. His verbal blades cut the deepest. He said I stunk, and my body was an embarrassment. I had awful breath, and I should never kiss anyone. He informed me my teeth were crooked, and that I should never smile with my teeth showing. According to Beau, I had no manners, and I was unruly and uncouth.

And all the while, he claimed I was lucky he'd wasted his time trying to polish me. After one nasty fight, he declared women knew their place back in the 1950s. Men didn't tolerate their insolent behavior back then. He assured me I would've been beaten to death or shunned, labeled a spinster. You don't realize until it's too late that you've stopped thinking for yourself under that kind of duress. It's like hiding in a trench in the middle of a war zone, with no weapons. You curl up into a ball, hoping it will end.

Beau had convinced my brain that his words were mine. He knew what was best for me, and I better listen. It's what I imagined people living in a cult experience. How I got to that point is not as relevant as learning how to escape it. I can't speak for everyone, but the first step for me was to find the seeds of confidence and be patient while they grew.

There are so many victims who wind up abused, male and female. They all had so much potential at some point in their lives. The one common thing to understand about anyone who's endured abuse is the chains of fear. The abuser provides the material to the abused, then teaches them how to make their own shackles.

When we pulled into the parking lot, all the fears paraded through my mind like the wild Mardi Gras in my hometown. But instead of tossing out beads and candy, my hands were full of fear and anxiety. I was convinced I would get in more trouble somehow with Beau if I proceeded with my plan. I worried I would never be loved again. Which is ironic because I was never loved the entire time Beau and I were together.

Then the rest of the fears joined the party. I was afraid of being alone, afraid that I would never make a decent salary again. I lacked a college education in my field or any other. I allowed Beau to manipulate me and isolate me from the beginning. I allowed him to take parts of myself that I was saving for someone worthy. He stripped me bare of my creativity and independence. I didn't even write poetry anymore. I stopped reading books. I actually became terrified of setting goals or planning for a better life. The painful reality of broken dreams was too harsh to take, so I stopped dreaming. I prayed many times to a God that I didn't even know: "If you are listening, please take me away from this Earth."

I didn't even pray for happiness or for God to change Beau. I prayed for death. There is no darker moment for a human being. I no longer judge others for whether or not they decide to stay or leave a dangerous situation, because sometimes staying is just as dangerous as running. I pray more now. I pray for any man or woman who has or is going through even a fraction of the trauma and pain I endured.

What I went through was real. But the day I had to speak with the lawyer, I doubted my story was believable. Truth is stranger than fiction, so they say. Though most of what Beau did to me was orchestrated to stay in the dark, to protect him and his reputation. I wanted and I needed the truth to come to light, even if that meant I would be placing myself in danger. I was in danger either way. And I worried one day I could be charged with a crime if the company uncovered his wrongdoings.

My fists were clenched while I tried to summon the courage.

"Are you okay?" my mother said, gently caressing my arm.

She had no idea I was losing the war that was unfolding in my mind.

You'd be surprised how many people overlook the significance and power of the human touch. It can have devastating effects when harm is intended. Yet it can be the most beautiful and healing gesture from those with love in their hearts. And love flowed through my mother's hand that day, giving me the boost I needed to win that war inside my mind.

I'll never forget how hard it was to open the car door that fateful morning. But I did it.

I tried to numb what I did not want to feel.
But the pain I felt, no medicine could heal.
Why you chose to wreck me
is something I'll never understand.
Was it something I brought on myself?
Or was it something that you planned?
When you promised me you'd change,
I clung on to every word.
While I was in a burning house,
saving someone I did not love,
I chose to see the good in you,

never asking myself why.
I guess what's normal to the spider
is chaos to the fly.

CHAPTER TWENTY-FOUR
Miracles on the Road

TWO MONTHS LATER, I found myself in a much better situation. I could finally see a clear path ahead of me. For the first time in my life, I was seeing the world for what it was and not through cloudy whiskey-colored glasses.

My mom stayed with me for four weeks and drove me to my daily appointments. And my attorney had a friend who offered me a job with a real estate agency in Knoxville. They needed an assistant office manager to coordinate all the sales and paperwork. I was entirely grateful for the assistance I was getting. I'm quite sure I would've relapsed those first two weeks if my mom hadn't been there for me, or if I didn't have something keeping me busy and full of purpose.

The medicine curbed the cravings, and it took a few weeks for the PTSD medications to kick in. I learned a lot during the outpatient sessions. It was fascinating to hear others' heartfelt descriptions of their lives and what led them to the same place. I prayed for all of them, and they prayed for me. I had been sober for more than four weeks, and I considered each day was a new record. But it wasn't easy. I was comforted to sit in a room full of people who listened to me and understood my disease. Likewise, I listened to each person's story with empathy. I had no idea a community of supportive people existed who struggled the same way I had.

The counselor had suggested on day one for my mom to remove all the alcohol from the house and to avoid going to places that had bars. If I wanted to positively change my life, I had to buckle down. And you don't know the limits of your willpower until you go to war with your addiction cycle. There were plenty of nights I begged my mother in tears to go buy one bottle of anything. But she stayed strong, and that helped me stay strong. For all those times as a child when my mother was never there for me, she had come back at the time when I needed her most. We bonded and rekindled a true mother-daughter friendship.

You have to participate in mental games to defeat alcoholism. I knew there would never be a day without me being tempted to drink. But each day I remained sober I chalked it up as a victory over Beau. By the third week, I was feeling better about myself. The new job was waiting for me as soon as I was ready. The salary wasn't nearly enough for me to keep my house. So my mom and I passed the time packing and listening to music, watching movies in the background, or just sitting on the couch talking. There was no better healing for me than that.

Was it a coincidence my mom was able to devote so much time with me because she was retired and getting social security checks? Her finances had improved because the father I never knew had worked for the government and had passed to the next life. I still had no spiritual faith or an inclination of what happens when you die. I was happy for my mom that she had received something positive in the end. She started receiving a monthly check from the government on his behalf, and that facilitated her ability to assist me with groceries and bills. My life and my health were moving in a positive direction.

It's right about then I became nervous. The daily abuse from Beau had conditioned me to assume everything was going to blow up in my face and turn to shit. My mom had to get back to Shreveport and get her house ready. She wanted to make space for me in case my house sold and gave me the option to come home.

I wasn't sure what my plans would be whenever my house sold, but having the choice as a backup felt reassuring. It was a new feeling for me. I ran away from home like a leaf in the wind without a plan, let alone a backup. My only path had been running in the wild with the pack.

Even time was slow and recognizable. Other recovering alcoholics know what I mean. If you're drunk all the time, you lose your place in the day-to-day normality of this world. When I was with Beau, I was drunk morning, noon, and night. I rarely knew the time or the day unless it was a holiday. If not for my interest in holiday decorations, I wouldn't have had anything to celebrate.

Humans are creatures of habits. We have physical habits, but those are extensions of all our mental habits. Besides alcohol, there was another important habit I needed to break. Over the years of Beau's abuse, my brain had been conditioned to the falsehood he had wrecked my world, with no hope of recovery. As I sobered, I realized it had been my choices that led me to the near destruction of my life. Understanding I had wrecked my own world was a bitter pill to swallow. I took refuge knowing if I wrecked it, I could fix it.

But I knew I still needed help. And sometimes you have to listen for the miracle calling you to the right place or person. When my thoughts were subdued by the alcohol, I doubt I would have recognized a miracle even if it had clubbed me over the head. Speaking of which, I had read somewhere that in Old England the bishops would walk around with a cudgel as they went from town to town. If you wanted to be healed or asked for a miracle, you needed to give the bishop a few coins to receive your "healing" blow to the side of your head. The stars spinning in your eyes was a sign God granted your miracle. I was willing to pay the price for any chance to heal.

Stories like that always steered me away from the various organized religions. Not that I needed help steering away from something I knew nothing about, and I had an ignorant view that God was just a man in the sky who granted wishes if you were good. Watching childhood friends go to church when I was young showed me their families didn't seem any better for it. And with my family, I sensed something was missing. I didn't know my soul was my connection to God. I figured the hollow feeling was the addiction calling to me. Every morning started with the same question: *Will I fall off the wagon or stay sober today?*

There I was in my car, full of doubt and worry, when the most amazing thing happened to me. I had driven to the new job one morning to fill out paperwork and let them know what day I could start. On the way home, construction had rerouted me down a few roads I didn't know. On a Friday, overcast and breezy but still warm for autumn, it all happened. And I will never forget that day as long as I live.

I wasn't in a hurry when I came to the end of a road with no clue whether to turn right or left. But it was a moment for my anxiety to creep in. While debating where to go, my fingernails scratched along the steering wheel. To my right, the clouds parted just enough for some sunlight to poke through. That was good enough for me. Now that I was sober, I could recognize positive signs as well as the red flags I had trampled over through the years.

The road I chose was little more than endless fields on both sides for almost an hour. At an empty four-way stop, I wondered what to do and where to go. I was lost. The voice inside my head that always told me to drink had better advice when deprived of alcohol. *Look and see!*

Startled by the instructive voice, I looked through all my windows. I was the only car on the road at that moment. There was a horse farm to my left and cornfields to my right. If I stayed on the road I was going, there was a church up ahead. It was simple and beautiful, newly painted white. My anxiety wanted me to find a liquor store. The sober part wanted me to get a better look at the church. The sunlight that had previously poked through the clouds was gone. This choice was all mine. Just then, I remembered someone in treatment had asked the group, "Do I go right where nothing is left, or do I go left where nothing is right?"

I had never been exposed to church life, but in I went. I took small steps like a cautious archeologist exploring a new cave. I was so nervous, but my soul guided me inside, as if knowing what was about to happen. There were people in the church off to the side. Two doors had been propped open, with most of the people outside in a small courtyard.

As I approached, I saw what could only be described as a pristine white tub that could fit a giant. It was half filled with clear water. The shadows were thick and heavy in the candlelight because of the cloudy weather.

The pastor had his back to me. "Is there anyone else?"

Everyone outside had gathered near the door and stared at me. I wanted to run. I wanted a drink. But willpower kept me there. After years of torture to my body and my mind, I was inside a nondenominational church that just happened to be performing baptisms that day.

"Did you come here to heal?" the old pastor said with the friendliest smile you could ever find on a face. "What is your name, my dear?"

"Sadie Crowe," I said, barely able to talk. I shook his wrinkled hand and felt the warmth of his kind heart.

"Would you like to be baptized today, Sadie?"

"How do you know I haven't already been baptized?" Had I just sassed a man of God?

He chuckled and said, "It's been my experience that God works through us when we let him. Miracles do happen, Sadie. But you have to reach out to them like a ripe apple on a tree."

I'll never know what came over me, but I agreed to be baptized. It was my choice, yet it was like a play I couldn't stop. I can't really describe the feelings running through me. I knew I was being guided, but the addiction part of my brain was screaming in my head to run. I wasn't sure why the idea of God made me feel uneasy. I secretly wished I had a shot of whiskey to give me courage.

The water was surprisingly warm. I sat down in my clothes, though I'd taken off my socks and shoes. The people had reentered from the courtyard, wearing genuine smiles of kindness and encouragement. The ceremony began with simple words once the pastor told me the process. No one was going to believe I was doing this. I asked the lady closest to the tub to use my cell phone to take a few pictures.

She took three. The first was me sitting up, half submerged in the water. The pastor was next to me, holding my hand, reciting the ritual. The shadows still swirled in the room, but there was enough light coming through the doors for her to take clear pictures without using any type of flash. The second picture was of me completely under the water. I felt heavy under the water, and I prayed that the paster would be able to lift me back up. I was under the water for seconds, but it felt like time stood still. I remember a feeling washing over me similar to the anxiety I had felt my entire life, but it was different in a good way. I felt free, as if birds caged inside me finally had been let out, taking with them a lifetime of guilt and shame. The moment I was lifted out of the water I was crying hysterically, and I could not speak. This was unlike any emotion I had ever experienced, yet it didn't scare me. I felt alive. I felt connected to a higher power.

Everyone clapped as the pastor helped me up. They dried me with towels and hugged me while I cried. It's not like me to accept a hug from family, so for me to hug a stranger was brand new.

After thanking everyone, the lady handed my phone back to me. The second picture and third picture nearly caused me to drop the phone. While submerged, the lighting in the room was split in two, like the shadows were fighting a sunlight invisible to the naked eye. The third picture was me sitting up, fully baptized. And the shadows had retreated while I was bathed in light.

Everyone gasped when they saw the pictures. I remember looking out the doors to see the still overcast sky. It wasn't sunlight that had shined on me. It was God, hugging me with the love I had longed for my whole life. If that day wasn't a miracle, then someone tell me what one is. I had truly emerged out of the darkness and into the light.

Out of the darkness and into the light.
This is my story; this is my fight.
I found God on the side of the road
while delegating others to help carry my load.
Though I did not know him, he did not forsake.
He just took with him what was his to take.
I was never meant to carry my sins.
It all washed away with the water on my skin.
I was trusting a process blind, without knowing
of where I just came from and where I was going.

CHAPTER TWENTY-FIVE

As Luck Would Have It

I DUBBED MYSELF A RETIRED BLACKOUT ARTIST. At least I could find the humor in what once scared me for my life. Being a blackout drinker is terrifying. There were many mornings I would run to the driveway and check for dents in my car while praying there wouldn't be blood on the grill from hitting something or someone. I tried my best not to drive when I was in that condition, but when I ran out of alcohol all bets were off.

Now I had a new chapter in my life to consider. It was wonderful and empowering at the same time. I'd been given a miracle from God and a second chance. And I wasn't going to waste it. My family and friends, especially Maw-maw, were shocked I got baptized. When I shared all the photos, everyone told me I was an inspiration. Me, an inspiration? I had never imagined such a thing could happen to me. It was a wonderful emotion to play with in my heart and soul. Was I on a lucky streak? Or was this what it meant to be healing in God's good graces? It took me quite a while to learn the difference.

I've discovered when you focus on positive feelings and events in your life anything can be possible. Good things will happen. Three days into my new job, I was experiencing relief and happiness. Then I received good news from my lawyer. It turns out I did have a case against my former employer. Not just a small case either. I had a big, fat case.

"They want to settle, Sadie," Andy said. "They haven't given me a dollar amount yet, but they know we mean business. I made it clear you would testify and make things incredibly ugly for the company."

I was speechless. Getting rich quickly wasn't even a thought nor was this my initial goal. I didn't walk into the attorney's office that day with any other intention than to protect myself. I wanted someone to hear what happened to me. I wanted someone to see what had been done to me. I had hoped the company would assist me with the bills and relocating until the house sold. I had been wrongfully terminated and wished for a letter of recommendation so I could find work elsewhere. Mostly, I wanted protection against Beau if he tried blaming me for all his illegal activities when I worked for him.

Because I was ignorant of employee rights, Andy methodically laid out all the laws Beau and the company had broken over the years.

"Sadie, are you still there?"

"Yes, I'm sorry, Andy. I'm just trying to soak everything in."

"Good. We have a lot to discuss," Andy said. "Let's start with how much money you think you're worth. Imagine that amount, and we'll add tax."

I didn't feel like I was worth very much in the mental state I was in. But I knew my story was worthy of being heard. Due to legal provisions, I'm unable to disclose the amount of money Andy planned to ask for on my behalf. It was more than I could've dreamed.

"We can get at least twice that if we take them to court," Andy said.

My blood froze. "I don't want to be in the same room with him. I'm not strong enough to see him face-to-face."

Andy sighed. "I understand. I'll haggle out an offer, but I want you to at least think about taking this to court. They owe you a lot of money."

"Thanks, Andy. But this isn't about the money. I just want to go home. I want to move on with my life. I want to pay off my debt to the hospital and the rehab center. And I don't have any insurance. I just wanted to have some money to get back home and not have to sell my car. I can barely keep my head above water."

"You'll get enough to do that and more," Andy said with a confident tone. "If you change your mind about going to trial, you'll wind up with a much bigger egg for your nest."

I thanked Andy again before we hung up. For me, it was a no-brainer. Take the money and run. I refused to go to trial. We settled out of court a few days later. And when the check came, I stood by the mailbox, wondering if it was real. I got in the car and took it to the bank before any leftover bad karma could set it on fire. It was enough to pay off my house, my car, all my other debts, and had plenty to stick in the bank. My mother was my first call to let her know the good news. I'll admit I was hesitant at first because my life taught me that everyone wanted something from me, and I was afraid she would want me to pay her for helping me the months she'd stayed with me.

"I'm so happy for you, Sadie-Cat," she said. "You stay sober, and I can pop back up there if you need me to." That was it. She did not want anything from me other than for me heal and to stay sober. I cried tears of joy like never before. Great things were happening to me. And I could never have imagined I'd have my mother back in the purest of ways. I had a new job and enough money to stow away and maybe start my own business one day. Reese was my second call. She had been a big part of why I was still alive, whether she knew it or not. It was vitally important to me that she and I could hang out together and didn't have to drink to have fun. And I continued with my appointments and tried my best to stay sober.

Being around people who don't judge you is an important thing when you're fighting an addiction. With each passing day, I started to become more of my true self. I remember sitting on my couch one evening. The house was quiet, and so was the voice in my head. I thanked God out loud for helping me make it this far.

Then another thing happened that would make me remember that night forever. I decided I was strong enough to go to a restaurant and take myself to dinner. There was a steak house I had wanted to try out ever since I got my new job. It wasn't far. When I reached the hostess station, I realized I didn't want to sit at a table and eat alone. But I also didn't want to sit at the bar for the obvious reason of not wanting to be tempted to drink.

I was about to walk out the door and took one last glance behind me. On the farthest side of the bar, a handsome man caught my attention. The yellow light on the wall behind him made it look like he had a golden glow around him. *Was it a sign? Was this a trick to get me to drink again?*

The man was dressed in a suit, a little too fancy for the steak house, so I figured he had to be a lawyer just getting out of work. I took a deep breath, said another prayer to God, and placed myself with one seat between us.

I was nervous. And it wasn't because I was sitting at a bar. And that's how I knew I'd be okay. I laughed realizing I'd never wanted someone to talk to me and ignore me at the same time before that night. The man seemed invested in the menu and hadn't even looked up at me after I had been sitting for more than five minutes.

The bartender handed me a menu. The wine selection caused my mind to race. I started to salivate for alcohol. It was a dangerous moment. I closed the menu and forced myself up with the intention of leaving. That's when he said something.

"Good evening. How are you?"

"I'm well," I replied, with my face already blushing. I couldn't remember blushing since I was a teenager.

"What's good here?" he asked me, assuming I'd eaten there before. "I would be honored if you sat with me . . . if you are alone, of course. I'll even pay for your dinner if you help steer me toward a delicious meal. This isn't my normal place, but something drew me here tonight."

Was God working another miracle?

Three long seconds of blushing went by before I spoke. What was wrong with me? I had never been this shy around anyone before. "Everything is probably good here. It is similar to one of my favorite places back home. I was feeling a little homesick, so I decided to check it out."

He gave a pleasant laugh as he stood up. He reached for my

hand like a true gentleman, as if we were in some movie. "My name is *Austin*. We could sit over at that table, if you'd like."

"I'm *Sadie*." He made my lips quiver, so I followed him to the table.

There was a polite husky tone to his voice. "You said you were homesick. Where are you from?"

"Louisiana," I said. Our eyes were locked in the most beautiful way.

We spent the next hour talking and laughing. I couldn't remember the last time a man had made me laugh so much. Austin was caring and confident without being cocky or arrogant. And when we had almost finished our meals, we were both quiet. I began to wonder if I'd insulted or embarrassed him. I worried my breath stunk like Beau used to tell me. My insecurities had their place inside me still, but I did my best to hide them from this wonderful stranger.

"I don't want to sound too forward," Austin said, locking his eyes on mine again. "But I have had a really great time getting to know you tonight. Can I see you again?"

"Sure," I said, wondering if I was acting cool or like a schoolgirl. I didn't want to give off the excited, overeager impression I was feeling inside. "I would like that very much."

"Here's my card. Just text me your number, and I'll plan something for us." He stood up and walked behind my chair to help me up. He was direct, but in a gentlemanly way, not a pushy way. He took control of the conversation and never left me wanting more. He was *all* man.

I was too enamored with this stranger to remember if I offered to pay for my meal or if he paid for the whole thing in a secret shake with the waiter. As he held the door for me, I looked at his card. He was a physical therapist, not a lawyer. I texted a short-and-sweet message when I got home. "This is Sadie. It was a pleasure to meet you, and I look forward to our next outing."

It took a while for me to go to sleep. I didn't hear from him until the next day, but he was already planning our second date. It had been so long since anyone showed me any kind of interest, and the butterflies in my stomach let me know it was genuine.

We arranged to see each other again in two days. Austin suggested we go somewhere we could relax and be playful, so we ended up at Dave and Busters. The second date started out even better than our first. The conversation was upbeat and flowing, and his compliments kept me in a constant state of blushing. It's a special feeling when your cheeks hurt from smiling so hard for so long.

The next thing I knew we found ourselves inside a video game box, and Austin kissed me. It was sweet, simple, and bold. It was exactly what I needed it to be. He was tall and strong. He was built well and in much better shape than me. He had salt-and-pepper hair and some gray growing into his well-manicured beard. He was rugged and sophisticated at the same time. Not only did he look good in a suit but I could tell he wasn't afraid to get his hands dirty either. To say I was intrigued and impressed doesn't do my feelings justice. In just two dates with Austin, I felt more alive than I'd felt with anyone else.

Back at the table, I confessed to him that I felt like he brought me back from the dead and that I haven't been out of the house in months. Over the next several weeks, we found ourselves spending a lot of time together. I loved getting to know him. Being wanted and desired was new territory for me. And Austin never missed an opportunity to compliment me or brush against me. I never would have imagined after all that I had gone through mentally that I would be this clever at flirting, but he made it easy.

Thanksgiving was approaching, and my garage was full of holiday decorations. We hadn't really discussed plans for our future. It was way too soon for that. Austin knew I was considering moving back home to Shreveport. I was overly cautious about my past. He made it clear it would be safe to tell him anything without fear of judgment, but he didn't push, and I didn't offer.

We were both content that I only showed him the parts of me that I thought a man would feel proud to show off in his potential partner. But I still had a black cloud of doubt looming over my head. I worried that one day Austin would notice all the flaws Beau had incessantly pointed out, and he would reject or abandon me. I was afraid he would ghost me if he thought I was too hard to love.

There were moments when I braced for Austin to insult me or stand me up, but he never did. He was so gentle with me, almost as if he could see how fragile I was. I didn't want him to realize I was hanging on by a thread most of the time we spent together. He had no idea that one raised tone or swift movement from his hand could put me in shell shock. Luckily, he never did either of those. He was purposeful when he spoke to me and always kind.

We continued seeing each other and kept the conversations fun and lighthearted. It took a long time before I told him I started falling in love with him after our first kiss. He made me feel safe, and he made me feel worthy, two things I yearned for the most. Austin coming into my life wasn't luck. He was another miracle from God.

Do you believe in fate?
Like somehow you ended up right where you belong,
despite the years of turmoil you've endured.
From living your life all wrong,
nothing could stop this unknown force.
It was always meant to be.
Darling, when you think of fate,
I hope you'll always think of me.
I never would have chosen this path.
But it's almost as if someone knew
that leading me down these forgotten roads
would end with loving you.

CHAPTER TWENTY-SIX
Spilling My Guts

I WOKE UP EARLY ONE MORNING, but this time it was not because my body needed a drink. I woke up that particular morning with an overwhelming sense of gratitude. It felt like a walking miracle to be alive, considering my ordeal with Beau. I could see all the positive aspects God had brought into my life. My mother and I had rekindled a relationship that was healthy for both of us. I was dating an amazing man, who happened to be everything I could want in a relationship. I had two good friends I could count on in Abby and Reese. I loved my new job, coordinating things for the Realtors out in the field. And my finances were in perfect order.

As awesome as all those things were, the biggest reason to be grateful: I was sober. I had discovered a higher power was watching over me. I didn't learn until later that believing in a higher power and having a spiritual awakening were components of the Alcoholics Anonymous 12-step program. I was truly blessed. As I sat there contemplating how much things had changed, I knew I was going to have to be vigilant for the rest of my life to keep this happy streak going. I prayed for strength not to drink when I woke up. Then I thanked God for each day I didn't drink before I went to bed. But I prayed to God even harder every time temptation came along, never forgetting that I needed God just as desperately on my best day as I did on my worst day. And it seemed that temptation was always brought on by anxiety and my PTSD. That wasn't something I could just pretend wasn't there. The therapist encouraged me to embrace the truth and to face it in my day-to-day activities.

To win the war against any addiction, you need to break down each day into manageable battles. Every day, every hour, and every moment was a mental skirmish. And after a lifetime of being drunk every day without fail, it was incredibly difficult for me. One mistake and that could be all she wrote for my happy life I'd been given. You need two things, in my opinion: You need to surround yourself with people who know and support your sobriety without judgment. That creates a stable playing field. Second, you must be proud of yourself when you win every battle. I know I'm not perfect, but Michelangelo once said something along the lines of, "You can't attain perfection if you don't aim for it." I think about that a lot. I had to be perfect, but I knew I was a frail human with a checkered past.

There are many people who went through less than I had and never made it out alive. Yet I was one of the lucky few who escaped and lived to tell the tale. That's why sharing what I've been through is so important to me. Looking back on the trauma Beau inflicted on me over the years, I'm baffled I still try to defend his actions. In my weakest moments, I still blame myself for what I went through. As I heal, I catch myself so I can stop giving energy to negative patterns.

Sometimes I think about his ex-wife, Caroline. I left Beau mentally many years before I left physically, but it took me over eight years to do that. Dating Beau had me thinking about the dreams I once had regarding marriage and children. It was difficult to imagine what she had gone through. And their kids must have been scarred for life. I never considered all the times she cried herself to sleep over something I said or posted or did. I asked God for forgiveness as I tried to take the next steps in my recovery. More than anything, I had to forgive myself and love myself again.

Caroline stuck it out with Beau longer than I ever could. At the end of it all, I have often wondered if it would help her if I called to apologize. There was always the possibility I'd make it worse, so I never did. Beau had lived the best of both worlds, which still wasn't enough.

I made a vow to myself while I lay there in bed that morning. I swore that I would never put another woman through that hell. Most of the blame fell on Beau, but there was still plenty of blame that fell on my decisions and inaction. I prayed constantly for Caroline and me to never have to experience anything like that again. I hoped she and her children found a happier path—the way I did.

I got dressed on that Saturday morning, prepared to go to the grocery store. I had my own cappuccino maker and needed more supplies. It was a tasty and safer alternative to whiskey. As I got in the car, Austin called. My heart was all a flutter. I know—totally mushy. But that's what he did to me every time I heard his voice.

"Do you want to meet for breakfast?" he asked in his devastatingly husky voice.

"Sure!" My smile came through the phone.

We met up at a little local dive we liked. He talked about his business and family matters while I soaked it all up. I couldn't get enough of him.

"What do you mean you have never owned a dog?" Austin asked in total disbelief. "You say hello to more animals than you do people every time we go for a walk."

"Well, I've always wanted a dog, but my family liked cats. My ex despised animal hair." The truth was, Beau hated all hair, which was ironic because he was balding terribly and had spent over ten grand for a laser hair removal for his back that didn't work. I never told him I noticed, of course. It would escalate and become a fight. Plus, I was the opposite of him. I didn't kick people when they were down. I felt a heavy sense of compassion for all who suffered. Beau hadn't aged well. His stringy, thin hair and bulging eyes made him look more like a Muppet. He was nothing like Austin, who had aged like a fine wine, broad shouldered and manly.

"Are you okay?" Austin asked, interrupting my mental recordings. "I hope I didn't bring up any bad memories."

I smiled and felt the heat on my cheeks. "You see that? You are exactly what I have been looking for. You care about me—maybe more than I care about myself."

Austin stared into my eyes. "You deserve to be loved, as we all do. And I know you have been through a lot, but I'm so grateful our paths led to where we are right now."

"Me too."

"If you could have any kind of dog in the world, what kind would you adopt?"

"Oh, I like this game." I put my finger up to my mouth as I thought. "I would love a little white dog, any kind, just a little fluffy, white, sweet fur angel."

"That's not a type of dog you know?" he said with a chuckle.

"I know, but they are all so sweet and cute. I don't know anything about dog breeds and personalities. I would be happy with whatever. But I don't think adopting a dog would cure my loneliness. And if I do decide to move home with my mother, my entire family hates dogs."

Austin sipped his coffee and smiled.

Whatever question he asked, my answer was always okay with him, a gentleman through and through. Part of me wanted to spill my guts about my past. I already trusted him that much, but I didn't want to spoil any of our moments. And everyone one of them had been fabulous. Not only that but he never pressed for it. He said on more than one occasion it mattered more to him who I was now. But it was important for him to see the old me that led me to the new me. I just wasn't ready to divulge that information yet.

The next day provided me with another pleasant surprise. Abby had secretly flown in to visit me. We had last discussed her coming the next month for Thanksgiving; then I would go to her place to spend Christmas and New Year's with her. I was happily surprised when she pulled into my driveway.

I couldn't wait to tell her about all that had been happening, especially Austin. We drove to the store and got the snacks and classic movies we both loved. Abby and I were comfortable being homebodies when we hung out. And that was safe for me. We always had an easygoing, low-maintenance friendship. We could go a month without speaking, then pick up right where we left off with no hesitation. We talked over the movies, as always. And

I explained to her how I'd miraculously stayed sober for months.

"It's amazing how much easier it is to heal being away from toxic people and stress. And it's a lot cheaper than therapy," I said with a giggle.

She laughed and went on telling me how proud she was of the changes I had made. She confessed how worried she was whenever she vacationed with me and Beau. And she couldn't figure out a way to bring it up without making things worse.

That's one of the biggest problems for people involved in abusive relationships. Victims are too embarrassed and frightened to reach out. And the family and friends who can sense what is going on don't know how to intervene. This has to change if the world is going to heal.

Abby didn't know what went on behind closed doors. I rarely shared that part of my life with anyone, apart from therapists and my attorney. Even then I didn't feel comfortable speaking about all the ugly aspects. For the same reason an adult brain blocks out trauma from childhood, my trauma made it easier to keep out of sight and out of mind.

At first I wasn't going to tell Abby anything and keep our visit a happy event. Yet my soul knew it was safe with her around. I told Abby everything I had been through, stopping only to wipe away tears. She sat and listened until I was done.

When Abby started to tear up, she reached over and hugged me for long minutes.

"I wish you would have told me, Sadie." Abby was a lot like me in the sense that we had difficulty expressing emotions to others. "I feel like such a bad friend for not stepping in."

"You have nothing to blame yourself for," I said. "And back then, if you tried to stand up for me, I would've stopped you. It was bad enough what Beau was doing to me. But there was no chance in hell I would've let that spill over on to you as well."

Abby gathered herself and started singing. We were quirky that way and handled drama in the same fashion. She sang the Chicks' song "Goodbye Earl." It was her way of showing me that Beau belonged in a hole somewhere.

I let out an uncomfortable laugh because I knew part of her meant that. Abby had a fiery spirit and was a fierce defender of her friends and family. She's still my biggest cheerleader and part of the reason I stayed alive long enough to escape. It was a great comfort to me to have such a strong woman in my corner, backing me up.

Abby wasn't the type of person who would try to stop you from making bad decisions or give an *I told you so*. Throughout our lifetime, she would wait until it was all over and catch me whenever I fell, only to remind me that I'm no better or worse for making the mistake in the first place. I loved and respected that quality.

Now that I had spilled my guts, I turned to the happier times I was experiencing.

"So what do you think I should do about Austin?"

"Follow your brain, Sadie."

"My brain?"

"Yes, your brain. Your heart clearly only likes to follow losers." Abby kept a firm look on her face.

"Touché," I said with a nod.

We have wandered aimlessly around this little town.
We sang into the bottles we couldn't put down.

We danced on tables and danced in the rain.
We numbed our emotions and drank through the pain.
Though I was reckless, you would never condemn.
Now and always my best friend.

CHAPTER TWENTY-SEVEN

All Is Fair in Love and War

They say that a dog is man's best friend, and that diamonds are a girl's best friend. Well, I must have done something right because I received both for Christmas. To my amazement, Austin had adopted the most beautiful, little white fluffy dog for Christmas.

"See? They do exist, exactly as I described her!" I said. I picked her up, and she licked my face, and I rubbed her soft puppy fur on my cheek. "I love her sparkly collar. What does the little ball on the collar say?"

"Lucky. That's her name."

"She's adorable."

"You both are," Austin said with a content grin. "I want you to stay in Tennessee."

My heart pitter-pattered again, but I tried to play coy. "I will admit you've grown on me."

"Why don't you move in with me?" Austin pushed away the fallen bangs from in front of my eyes.

"We've only known each other six months," I said, becoming nervous.

"When you know, you know, Sadie. This feels so right to me. I know you feel it too."

"Of course I feel it too. But you haven't heard about my past. You might feel differently if you knew everything."

"Unless you tell me you're an escaped convict wanted for murder, I doubt anything you tell me would change my mind."

Before the ghosts of my anxiety scared me into silence, I spent the next two hours telling Austin everything about me. He listened without interruption, sitting on the opposite side of the couch while I rubbed Lucky's ears. Thank God for that little puppy. Though I half-expected him to show me the door, I trusted my brain like Abby had suggested. I decided if I was going to tell him, he might as well get it all. He learned about my childhood, drinking at an early age, running away from home, bartending, my life with Beau, my trauma, and even my suicide attempt.

I was stoic at first, but by the end I was bawling. Lucky didn't understand and licked my face, which helped.

"I admire you for being so strong," Austin finally said. "Most of the people I meet deny their past. You recognize your faults and want to improve. And that takes courage and wisdom."

"Thank you," I said as he handed me a Kleenex. I never imagined I would feel so close to someone so quickly. I couldn't have dreamed up a more perfect man. And I felt weak and strong at the same time.

Lucky barked as we stood up and hugged. She continued

barking while we kissed.

"I guess it's Lucky's turn now," Austin said with a wry smile.

"What do you mean?"

We both sat down with the puppy between us. "Take a closer look at the silver ball on her collar."

It was reflective and smooth, with her name in the front. But there was a tiny latch on the bottom. I clicked it and out popped a ring. A diamond ring. It was stunning. I stared in disbelief while the diamonds sparkled like starlight. As I held the ring in my trembling fingers, I couldn't speak. I hadn't even noticed Austin was kneeling next to me.

"Will you marry me?"

The rest was history. My fairy tale had come true. After accepting, I suggested we have a long engagement. We could continue dating, and I would keep the house for a year. Then I could put it on the market. After that, we would figure out a date. I wasn't sure if he would agree to my plan, but I knew it would give me time to squash my anxiety.

He agreed, and we couldn't have been happier. His parents had passed, but we called my mom and Maw-maw, who were ecstatic. It's quite amazing what God can and will do in your life when you finally decide to let go of the negative things and people that should have had no place in your world to begin with.

The next few weeks were like heaven. I was still attending my weekly therapy sessions to remain sober. Sometimes we went out on the town. But we enjoyed staying home and making meals together. Whether we stayed at his house or mine, Lucky was always there, to my eternal joy.

As the months went by, I gained mental clarity and confidence.

I'd fallen in love with the man meant for me, and I had welcomed my new fur baby into my life. And I never wanted to be without them. Also, I no longer had to see Beau or think of him ever again.

I'll admit there were times I thought about how he got away with everything. After all the evil he had done and was likely still doing, he seemed to have escaped scot-free. So I asked God to help me understand how a person could inflict so much pain to so many people, wrecking the lives of innocents while nothing seemed to change.

I guessed it was no longer my battle to fight. It was no longer my burden to carry. Letting go never came easy to me. I carried things far longer than God intended me to. It's a deficiency of mine. Letting go means I had to somehow forgive him for everything and be at peace with it. Someone once told me that you will know when you are 100 percent over someone. It's the moment you have an opportunity to get revenge and you choose not to.

I wasn't there yet. And I wondered if peace would be unattainable in my scenario. Did I want revenge? I sure did. I wanted to see him cry in fear for his life and career. I wanted him to be at the mercy of me when I looked him in the eyes to say, "All is fair in love and war, baby." I could hear him in my head, calling me a dumb bitch and telling me I'd be sorry. I dreamt of the day I would get even, and he would regret underestimating me.

A call from my mother interrupted my inner soliloquy.

"Sadie-Cat, you won't believe it."

"What, Mom? Are you okay?"

"In the *Shreveport Daily* this morning, there's a front-page article on Beau and Spencer. They've been fired and indicted for embezzlement."

Anxiety is now fleeting.
And I'm gaining back my pride.
The tools have always been there.
They just haven't been applied.
Some days the rooms are busy.
And sometimes they are dim.
But I'm never without faith.
And I never lack a friend.

CHAPTER TWENTY-EIGHT
Patience and Vigilance

I WASN'T SURE HOW TO REACT to the news at first. Beau had been indicted. Would he face justice for all the things he'd done? I wondered if I should come forward in front of the public and tell the world about what really transpired. Wouldn't I feel vindicated if everyone saw the pictures of my bruised face and body? Vengeance was definitely flowing inside me.

I had a long talk with Austin. He wanted to defend my honor by taking Beau into a dark alley to give him a taste of what it's like to be left with a broken body on the pavement. But what was best for us became our priority. It had been a few years since I had even seen Beau. I had no idea that I wasn't the only one watching what he was doing. I was safe because of the legalities of my settlement.

Would I be safe if Beau thought I was a source of information behind his indictment? He had connections with nefarious people who wouldn't bat an eye at doing me harm. And I didn't want Austin to come to harm either. So we decided to watch from the stands and see how things played out. Trials of this nature usually took years.

Austin and I let the negativity drift away as we created a nest. We got married and even had Lucky in the wedding as the ring bearer. It was magical day for both of us. And I fulfilled a wish to marry a wonderful man who I knew would always put me first. I'm a giver, and so is he. Nothing could stop our love. Austin had been attentive and incredibly patient with me, especially when my anxiety nearly got the best of me leading up to the wedding.

It was an outdoor ceremony in early autumn. We made it a dry reception, which made me feel guilty. I wanted everyone to have a good time and not change their habits because of my situation. This is just one of the many things that run through the mind of a recovering alcoholic.

My mother and Maw-maw came to Tennessee. Abby and Reese were there as well, and that settled me down. Though it was a small wedding, I carried myself like a movie star, strolling down the aisle of flowers. It was a whirlwind of fun. Austin and I danced for hours before we left for our honeymoon. We promised we would open the presents and cards when we got back.

Croatia was gorgeous, and we had perfect blue-sky weather the entire week. Austin was an avid sailor and taught me how to sail during the day. Each night we dined on fantastic food in front of roaring waves. It was perfect.

The following months were hectic for both of us. We decided to buy a new house, so we had two houses to sell, we had our jobs, and I still had to go to counseling and AA meetings. The high-anxiety days for me challenged my resolve. Austin's unwavering support always made me feel like I wasn't alone. I had a true partner. And so did he. Sometimes I'd question if the life I found myself in was real. I physically pinched myself to make sure I wasn't in some delusion. If I could make it this far, given my background and how low I had sunk, I knew it was possible to keep things moving in a happy direction. Patience and vigilance would be my fuel.

I'll admit there were mornings I woke up wondering if Beau would wind up in jail. And I hoped he would. As time went by, I realized the fight against my PSTD and the addiction would never go away. The appointments with counselors and AA groups encouraged me to be a strong and sober human. Don't let anyone tell you attending those are a waste of time. If you're willing to ask for help, you can improve your situation. That's what recovery is all about, in my opinion. Improving each day as much as you can.

I even became a churchgoer. Austin was strong in his faith and his relationship with God. I prayed so many times to my God, as I knew him, and it was like having a friend devoted to me and my well-being every second of the day, no matter where I was or what I was thinking.

For addicts in recovery, having a lifeline to a higher power full of love is vital to be sober and remain sober. The toughest thing for me was facing the fact that God is perfect, and I am not. The human ego has a way of making you think you can do anything. That's when you lose your footing and find yourself rolling down a hill.

There was a particular moment of temptation for me one day after work. I was tired and hadn't slept much. I was shopping for the dinner Austin and I had planned to make that night. At the time, I had no idea why I was feeling overly emotional. I passed by an endcap that had one of my favorite whiskeys. *Buy one, get the second half off!*

Now some people see that as Satan tempting a soul in a time of weakness. I see it as just an everyday battle that a recovering alcoholic mind creates on its own. It's my belief that Satan only has power if it's given to him, whereas God has all the power regardless of what you do.

I said a prayer, took a deep breath, and skipped to the next aisle. I felt good about myself until I realized I still needed to go back that way for something on my list. The thought of having a drink again was potent. I was in a vulnerable situation, and I knew it. My hands shook when I picked up one of the bottles. If I just held it and looked at it, maybe it would help me get past it. Then I put it in my cart. Then I put another one next to it.

I pulled out my phone to call Austin. It went straight to voicemail. He was seeing patients that afternoon. I didn't say anything and hung up. *What should I do if he calls back? Should I tell him? I could hide them in the shoe closet. He'd never know. I don't have to open the bottles. If I didn't drink, what was the harm? What if we have guests for a party, and they wanted to drink? I shouldn't make other people change their behavior because of me!*

My mental gymnastics were still capable of convincing me I was doing the right thing as I approached the checkout. And then my phone rang. I knew it was Austin. I didn't answer. The cashier put everything into bags and gave me the total. As she waited for me to pay, I realized I had left my purse in the car.

"Hold on. I'll be right back," I said with a frantic tone.

I jogged out to the car and got in. When I grabbed my debit card, my phone rang again. It was Austin. This time I answered.

"Hi, Sadie. Sorry I missed your call. Is everything okay?"

I couldn't answer. I was shaking; then I started crying.

Somehow that wonderful man knew. "Where are you?"

"At the Food Mart." That was all I could manage to say.

"You stay right there. I'll meet you in five minutes."

It was three minutes. I got out when he pulled up, and we hugged while I cried. I told him what happened, and he took me home. We went back for my car later that night. He praised me for reaching out for help in a moment like that. We ordered a pizza and turned it into a fun night.

I was proud of myself for not going back in and buying the whiskey before he got there, but shame hung over me because I almost failed in a big way. The fear had gripped me. I prayed for more patience and more resolve. I knew staying sober was not always going to be this hard, but for now, I needed to use the tools I had been given. *Just for today.*

The next morning I discovered the source of my emotional turmoil the day before. I was pregnant.

"You said you wanted children," Austin said, holding me while he stood behind me. "But I thought we'd have plenty of time before we struck gold."

We both laughed. He had such unique way of seeing the bright side or diffusing tension. I didn't have a single craving while I was pregnant. I knew the damage it could do. There are extra hormones a pregnant mother receives that qualify as survival necessities. Every day I thought, *What's good for me is good for the baby. And whatever is harmful for me could be catastrophic for the baby.*

When that little girl was in my arms, the rest of the universe melted away. I thanked God she was healthy. And even though I felt like a giant marshmallow, the pain of labor and worries leading up to it were worth the amazing moment.

"You're both so beautiful," Austin whispered, standing over us. "You did great."

I could tell he'd been crying. He admitted he couldn't stand the thought of hearing me cry out during the labor. He had felt helpless.

"We are a beautiful family," I said with a calming smile. "Thank you for making all my dreams come true."

"Which of the three names are you picking for her?" he asked. We had selected them so it would be easier when the moment came.

I looked in her blue eyes and said, "Lilly."

"Lilly it is."

I fell asleep with my baby girl in my arms.

She was my Wonder Woman.
And boy, you should have seen her fly
through the house in seconds.
If she ever heard me cry,
nothing could ever hurt her.
She wasn't afraid of much.
She had such intimidating features,
with such a gentle touch.
She never got any older.
To me, she'll always look the same.
She endured trials in her life, but she wouldn't change a thing.
I used to think when I was sleeping
she would fly around the moon.
But all my dreams were fairy tales,

and I grew up way too soon.
I wondered if I could be like her.
For the one I had in my arms,
to protect with all her toughness
and love with all her charms.

CHAPTER TWENTY-NINE

Slipping in the Shadows

After more than six years away from Beau, my life had drastically improved. I prayed every day in appreciation for my husband and my daughter. And, of course, Lucky. Austin was the epitome of what a God-fearing, faithful, and honest man should be. Occasionally, my PTSD still had me question why he loved me. The scars from abuse are not easily healed. And I wonder if all the damage done to me can be overcome.

I've often thought trying to remain sober was like walking a tightrope. And I wondered how I had become an acrobat, skilled enough to walk over the fire without falling. Thinking you have made it across safely is the most dangerous thought an addict can have. Overconfidence and ego are the secret assassins. You can't let your guard down for a single second. That's how I viewed things until I actually did fall.

Self-doubt gnawed at me like rats chewing through the concrete of my house. I held them off until I thought they were gone. Little did I know, they were inside the walls. I had my weekly meeting with my addiction group. I went inside with my peers while my addiction waited outside in the parking lot. The therapy was great. It had helped tremendously. I learned from others and hoped they learned from anything I offered. I even made a few friends outside meetings who were also sober.

One of the days during lunch, I was supposed to meet one of my new friends. When I got there, she texted to cancel because she wasn't feeling well. Though disappointed, I headed to one of the tables near the windows to eat by myself.

Three of the women from therapy I didn't know as well had met up after the meeting and saw me. They invited me over to their table. It was fun. We talked and shared our opinions about some of the speakers we had listened to over the last month at AA meetings. The little gathering washed away the disappointment of my friend not showing up. I needed to use the bathroom, so I excused myself. I told them what I wanted in case the server showed up before I got back.

When I returned to the table, the ladies had all ordered wine. They were laughing and had already filled my glass. One of the AA steps is to *play out the tape*, which means to envision your high from your drinking and then remember the low that comes after. It's a great deterrent and a wise skill to have for remaining sober. But I didn't hesitate at all when I saw the wine or play the tape through. And that was the scariest part. I sat down, we all clicked our glasses, and finished the bottle before I had time to second-guess myself.

After the meal, we hugged and left. None of us were supposed to drink, not even a drop. At least in my case, but perhaps they didn't have as big of a problem as I did. I convinced myself I'd been so good for so long that I deserved a treat. How could one glass of wine hurt? Typically, it would take at least two bottles of wine for me to even get buzzed. I was certain I had healed to the point where alcohol would not be able to control me as it had most of my life.

I drove home, and the closer I got, the more guilty I felt. Austin wasn't home yet. He was picking up Lilly from day care. I ran in the house in a bit of a panic. *What if he smelled the wine on me?* I brushed my teeth and gargled. Then I threw my clothes in the washing machine. Then I got dressed and started to vacuum. Lucky yapped at me the whole time. I was frantic.

It didn't take long for Austin to suspect something was wrong that night. Though I didn't lie to him, he never asked me directly if I had taken a drink. I admitted I had a headache, and I needed a nap. Both were true. Then the voice returned. *You did nothing wrong.*

A few days later, when I was at the house, I found a bottle of whiskey hidden behind the old cupboard in the basement next to the dryer. I was shocked, wondering how it got there. I had no conscious memory of buying it or stashing it. Fear strangled me like a giant python. I ran up the stairs and shut the door. I had the day off from work because I had a counseling session in the late morning. I was alone. I paced the house asking myself how the bottle had gotten there. But I knew I must've done it. Austin certainly wouldn't have bought it or put it in the house. I had no recollection of hiding it there in the basement.

I told myself over and over to leave it alone. But the obsession consumed me. I could not coexist with alcohol. The next thing I knew, I was heading down the stairs again. I couldn't stop myself from opening it and drinking it right out of the bottle. It burned my throat. Yet it felt good, like an old friend. No, it was more like meeting up with a cellmate who shared a bunk with you in prison. I felt thrilled, buzzed, and horribly guilty all at the same time. Even the devil and angel on each of my shoulders began to dance with each other.

So there I was, drinking alone in the shadows of the basement. I'd lost control and knew it wasn't right, but it didn't stop me from taking the next swig. It didn't take long for me to drink the whole bottle either. That was scary too. I skulked around to see if there was any more buried treasure my mind had kept hidden from me. But that was it. I had a tight grip on the empty bottle, like a child with a pacifier. Then I talked to myself, trying to downplay what I had just done.

Lucky knew. She sat at the top of the stairs, looking at me. Accusing me. Pets are smart.

"This will be our little secret," I said. I received a pitiful whine in return.

After I took the bottle and the trash to the garbage bin, I looked at the clock. I had missed my appointment. And it was my turn to pick up Lilly at day care. I once lived most of my life as a functional drunk. Now that I slipped back into it, I took to it like a fish to water.

I drove slowly out of precaution. I went inside the day care, acting as if nothing out of the ordinary had taken place. I didn't see Lilly right away. She was outside on the swings with some of the other kids. The woman at the front desk of the day care greeted me as she always did. And I tried to keep my distance by claiming I might have a cold, a ploy that had worked for me in the past. I could feel myself sweating, though it was a chilly day.

Lilly ran across the room, and I held her hand as we got to the car. I couldn't remember if we talked or not. My memory lapses were getting worse, and I knew it. Once Lilly got settled in with her snacks in front of the TV, I thought I might've escaped the consequences of my failure.

Austin surprised me when he came home early. I could tell he was upset, both angry and sad. The day-care teacher called him. Apparently, my drunken state was obvious to the eyes and nose of a trained professional. My heart plummeted. I confessed everything to Austin, including that I had memory loss. I didn't know if he'd divorce me on the spot and take my precious little girl away from me. The defeat I felt inside was beyond measure.

Austin was stern yet kind while he helped me pack a bag because we had agreed the best thing to do was to check me in to a three-day inpatient recovery at the hospital. And he assured me that we could beat this addiction together. But we both knew I couldn't be a wife or a mother if I returned to a life of drinking.

I couldn't look at him as we drove. I had failed him and my innocent child. Austin and I were mostly upset for the same reason. I had endangered Lilly. I could've gotten in an accident. If Lilly had come to harm because of me, that would be more than I could endure. My renewed guilt conjured merciless thoughts of what people would say once they found out I'd fallen off the wagon.

When the whiskey wore off, I sat alone on the hospital bed and cried endless tears. I felt like I had ruined the treasured gifts God had given me. I didn't deserve happiness. Darkness was closing in again. I hated Beau for doing what he did to me. This was all his fault. Then the blame turned inward. I did this to myself. I was the one who had fallen from grace. I begged God for a second chance. I didn't feel like I deserved it, but I knew I couldn't win this war on my own.

Maybe that was what God had showed me. I needed the strength to ask for help for the rest of my life. The hardest thing an alcoholic must cope with is letting go of ego. And if I was going to make this better, I'd have to take ownership of my actions.

Responsibility doesn't have to be a solitary task. There are always available resources at all times—day and night—willing and able to assist those who have fallen and want to walk again. Acceptance of your actions is the first step toward recovery.

Failure isn't an easy thing to deal with in your mind, let alone sharing it with those who love you. And it is they who usually get hurt the most. I was ashamed and embarrassed in a way I had never felt before. As I walked into the house, I promised Austin and myself it would never happen again. The stakes were too high. It wasn't just my life anymore. I had to consider the two souls dearest to me. I had let everyone down. But I was determined to make it right.

I had to go back to step one. My new job was understanding of my situation and agreed to pay for a monthlong outpatient treatment that gave me access to good doctors, counselors, and therapy. As long as I attended each weekday and passed the drug tests, my job would be there for me. I was grateful for their assistance. It gave me time to regroup. I couldn't allow anything like that to happen again.

I've brought you on this journey and told you this story—for me. But I also told it for you and anyone you might know who could benefit from my life story. If you made it this far, maybe you were meant to tell others. If even one small thing you read helped you stay sober today, then God spoke to you through me.

My advice to anyone who is an addict or is struggling in an abusive situation that seems impossible to get out of—recognize you have strength inside you. Find it, nurture it, and set your soul free. I want you to know it can happen. I'm living proof. For those healing from addiction, abuse, PTSD, or clinical depression, it is likely you have or will come across the term *emotional dysregulation*. This is our battleground.

Don't let anyone tell you how you should feel in a given situation or that your emotional reaction isn't appropriate. We are imperfect beings striving for perfection or just trying to get to the end of the day. So go easy on yourself. Forgive yourself. Love yourself. Know that it's okay to feel overemotional in a situation. Allow yourself a chance to heal, no matter how long it takes. Seek help when you need it. Let go of what others think of you.

Share your fight with those you trust—family and friends. Let them know you're working on regulating your emotions. Embarrassment comes from worrying what others think. Happiness is letting go of worry. Just let your emotions come out as they are. Embrace them, feel them, and then let go of them, because there will be endless waves of emotions coming from inside you for the rest of your life. That's what it means to be human. Together we ride the waves of the ocean of emotions. The key is to find happy moments and successes wherever you can. If you look for them, you will find more sunny skies than stormy ones. And when you're in a storm, remember it will end, and the sun will shine again soon.

Make a journal of all the happy feelings you experience each day, then go back and read them at the end of the week. We aren't crazy, because we are healing. We're all emotional souls trying to reconnect with God. Tears of happiness and tears of sadness are equally important. The greatest tears are the bravest tears.

I danced with the devil again, but that is nothing new.
We danced together many times before I married you.
To pick it up or put it down was never hard to choose.
The truth is that it killed me then, but I had much less to lose.
I used to cry in the mirror, while in the bottle I'd drown,
before my biggest fear became letting my family down.
It had been several long years since the last time we danced.
He pulled me in and whispered as my mind romanced.
This time it would be different; this time it would free my soul.
He swore that if I drank this time I'd be in control.
Of all the nights I drank, followed by all the guilt and shame,
nothing compared to hurting my child,
and that has changed the game.
Thank you for your patience, and most of all your faith
that beyond this hurdle is a woman who hasn't lost her place.

Epilogue

I sat in the back of the courtroom with Austin on the morning of Beau's sentencing. Even though there was nothing that would link me or my name to the trials of Spencer and Beau, I wore a hat and sunglasses as camouflage.

Spencer received two consecutive jail sentences of seven years each for his racketeering, money laundering, and bribery. Spencer's countersuit was dropped due to the nefarious details that became known during Beau's trial. The weight of testimony given by accountants and staff who had come forward against Beau had been staggering.

I speculated that Beau had lied to his lawyer. That wasn't much of a reach, considering he had lied to everyone I ever saw him interact with. It was rumored the evidence Beau had hidden from the trial had made his lawyer furious.

The jury had spent less than an hour to deliver Beau's guilty verdict. I'll never forget the days leading up to the day of sentencing. The media speculated he was going to get the hammer. The judge in the case had a reputation for being extra hard on those who caused physical harm to women and lied in a courtroom. It really couldn't have gone any better. I didn't realize I'd been squeezing my supportive husband's hand so tight his fingers were numb.

I'd always wanted retribution of some kind. But as I sat there, waiting for the proceedings to begin, I wasn't sure what I really wanted to happen. Part of me wanted to stand up and tell the entire courtroom what Beau had done to me. And I wasn't the only one who had suffered abuse at his hands.

As I followed the story in the media, his fiancée had already left him because of a fight over him cheating on her that left her bruised. Julie didn't wait around for a second bout. She'd been wiser than me and had a lot more resources and options. And she never pressed charges on Beau either. Instead, she used social media to humiliate him. Her friends and family made it clear that if Beau came within a mile of her, he'd be the one buried in a hole in the middle of nowhere. Oh, the irony.

When the guards brought Beau in through the side doors, I could see the chains and hear them clanking as he walked. I later found out he'd already gotten into a fight with one of the cell guards. When the bailiff announced the judge entering the courtroom, tears welled at the corners of my eyes.

This is what I had always wanted. But it was surreal to actually witness it. My emotions were all over the place, but Austin's presence kept me steady. My mind was jumbled with all the memories of physical and emotional abuse I suffered. Then I realized the judge was speaking.

"I must say it's been a long time since I have presided over a case of this magnitude that focused on one individual's hubris and villainy." A hush fell over the courtroom. "Based on your past history, the testimony in this trial, and your former boss's trial, I would wager you have led a long life of abusive behavior and bullying tactics to achieve your goals. I wouldn't be surprised one bit if you had murdered someone along the way to succeed in whatever twisted schemes you ran with impunity. You, sir, are a snake."

The judge banged the gavel three times.

"On the two counts of corporate theft, I sentence you to ten years in prison for each. On the three counts of racketeering, I sentence you to fifteen years in prison, without parole, for each of those crimes. It is my hope you will never step one foot outside a prison for the rest of your life. All sentences will run consecutively. May God have mercy on your soul. This court is now adjourned."

I watched Beau's shoulders slump, but he didn't cry. Should I have felt sorry for him? I was relieved justice had finally caught up to him, but what he did to me could never be undone. Did I want to see him receive the same abuse he gave to me? Would I have felt better if he had been placed in a stockade in front of my house so I could throw garbage at him every day? It's hard to let go of the revenge I had wanted for so long. But knowing he would be imprisoned for the rest of his life closed an ugly chapter in my life. Part of me embraced the peace that filled me. The other part of me wanted to walk over to Beau and tell him with a grin, "If I'd played a part in your downfall, it would have been worse."

I suddenly recalled Beau saying, "I'd rather hang on the spot than go back to jail."

I walked out with my loving husband, thankful to be free of the drama, but I knew some scars would never heal. Did I want to go to a bar and drink? I did, but my love for Austin, Lilly, and myself was stronger than my temptation. I once thought God came into my life when I chose to be baptized. But that wasn't true. God had been with me my whole life.

When I study news and statistics on orphans and runaways, my survival and deliverance could only be owed to a higher power, not dumb luck. I had escaped death where many had not. I knew my purpose going forward was to enjoy life, cherish the gifts God had brought me, and to help others find their way to peace and freedom.

I don't know when it happened—the day I took back the control over my own life. It all happened overnight, it seemed. I woke up one morning and found myself free of the tyranny and the devotion to the pain giver. Beau was never the wolf in this story. Despite how many times he shredded me with his teeth and ate me alive with his words, he wasn't the wolf. The real predator in this story is and will always be alcoholism. Whiskey had been the very thing I used to numb my will and confuse my awareness that what I drank had caused me the most pain. Alcohol spun the vicious cycle of pain, abuse, and needing to be saved.

I also realized that neither myself nor Austin were the heroes in this story. I needed to be saved by a hero, but there was never going to be anything or anyone who could fill the God-size hole in my heart. Only God was able to save me. And in the end, he did. I was brought out of the darkness and into the light, given a second chance to see the world from a new perspective. This allowed me to use my divine purpose in life, and that was writing this story. If I can reach anyone who is going through similar trials, then I have won the war.

I no longer live in chains. I no longer allow abuse to take place in my life. And I don't let anyone steal my peace. The lessons I learned from my failures while drinking whiskey with the wolves taught me how to see beauty in the horror I was trapped in. I was resilient, and I survived even when I didn't want to. The only thing that mattered was that God had blessed me so I could survive.

My life has value no matter how cheap I felt and how cheap Beau made me feel. Austin saved my heart and brought me back to life.

Before I read my vows to him on our wedding day, I cried while holding the hands of my bridesmaids. I told them how I used to pray for God to make Beau honest and gentle. I'd prayed for God to change Beau into the man I needed him to be. But God couldn't change someone who was not willing to change. Instead of changing Beau, he allowed Beau to leave me. At the time it seemed like torture. But I see now God's beautiful plan was to replace Beau with the man I was praying for. He sent me a real man of God.

I once heard you can tell if you are in love with a man or woman of God if you can read successfully through 1 Corinthians 13:4 7–8 and replace love with your partners name. And at the end, find the message is still true. So I tried that.

Austin is patient. Austin is kind. Austin does not envy . . . and so on. And sure enough, it was all still true. Then I tried the same thing, inserting Beau's name. *Beau does not boast. Beau is not proud. Beau is not self-seeking . . .* and so on.

There it was, right in front of me. Beau didn't align with a single line of that prayer. That is the moment I knew God had heard my prayers. It took some time and recognition on my part to get away from Beau. God brought me the worthiest man because Beau was never going to be a Corinthians man, and that's okay. He and I were never meant to be together. All those years we spent trapped in the vicious cycle of lust, violence, and addiction only took us further away from our connection to God and our true purpose.

I forgive Beau for everything he put me through. It was detrimental for me not to forgive him for my own peace. If given the opportunity to seek revenge on him, I know now I wouldn't. I don't wish him or anyone else harm or ill will.

I drove away in my sports car that night with "Praying" by Kesha playing on my iPod, and I absorbed all the lyrics to her song. Rather than being bitter toward my past, I sang every word to that song loud and at peace. I meant every word:

I hope he is out there praying.
I hope his soul is changing.
I hope he finds peace
crawling on his knees
praying.

Resources

- *The Big Book of Alcoholics Anonymous*
- *Alcoholics Anonymous Big Book* (4th ed.). (2002). Alcoholics Anonymous World Services.
- National Suicide Prevention Lifeline The Lifeline provides 24-7 free and confidential support for people in distress, prevention and crisis resources for you or your loved ones, and best practices for professionals. If you're thinking about suicide, are worried about a friend or loved one, or would like emotional support, the Lifeline network is available 24-7 across the United States. You can call 1-800-273-TALK (8255) or chat.
- Crisis Text Line Text Line is free 24-7 support for those in crisis. Text 741741 from anywhere in the US to text with a trained crisis counselor. Crisis Text Line trains volunteers to support people in crisis. With over seventy-nine million messages processed to date, they are growing quickly, but so is the need.

- National Domestic Violence Hotline
  800-799-7233
  SMS: Text START to 88788

Substance Abuse Hotline

- SAMHSA's National Helpline, 1-800-662-HELP (4357) (also known as the Treatment Referral Routing Service), or TTY: 1-800-487-4889 is a confidential, free, twenty-four-hours-per-day, 365-days-per-year information service, in English and Spanish, for individuals and family members facing mental and/or substance use disorders. This service provides referrals to local treatment facilities, support groups, and community-based organizations.

- Also visit the online treatment locator, or send your zip code via text message: 435748 (HELP4U) to find help near you. Read more about the HELP4U text messaging service.

About the Author

Erica Spray is a Louisiana native who planted roots in sweet home Alabama. She now lives with her husband, Shane, and their son, Cooper. Writing has always been Erica's passion, and she is excited to share her love in *Whiskey with Wolves* and other forthcoming books.